MERRY ME

A DRAGONS LOVE CURVES STORY

AIDY AWARD

Cover by: Melody Simmons

For all my lovely readers and fans who asked me for a purple dragon, who begged for a purple dragon, who said "Wouldn't it be cool if there was a purple dragon?", who asked "Aidy, can't there be a purple dragon?", "Why aren't there purple dragons?"

Even though I said there was no such thing as freaking purple dragons.

FINE!

Here's your purple dragon!

You willed him into existence.

"I don't have a purple problem, I have a purple passion!"

— JACKIE HARMON SWEENEY

THE ICE MAN FOUNDETH

"*J*ingle balls, jingle balls, ice and snow can suck it." Genny was cold, snot ran down her face in icicles, and she was either going to die out here in the middle of nowhere Antarctica, or fail out of her Ph. D program.

She had never failed out of anything. She didn't plan to start now. So... death by hypothermia it was.

Professor McFuckface wanted samples of the bizarre black mineral they found in the ice where nothing but snow and frozen water should be. That's what she was going to give him. Even if her fingers froze, turned black, and fell off in the process.

As a bright-eyed and fluffy-minded college freshman, when she'd imagined getting her doctorate in volcanology, she'd dreamed of deserted tropical isles, with beaches at the base of rumbly peaks that poked out of the water in the far off reaches of the Pacific. Maybe those volcanoes sang songs about "I lava you", and maybe they had tribes of orange soda addicted natives looking for someone to sacrifice to the Big Woo.

Not once had she dreamed of having the hairs on the inside of her nose freeze just because she deigned to breathe. She also hadn't anticipated weeks of inappropriate man jokes from her fellow scientists that bordered on sexual harassment simply because she was... gasp... a woman in STEM. But both were her current reality.

And yes, for the record, her vagina was currently frozen shut.

Genny stabbed her pick into the wall of ice she'd been chipping away at. "Stupid Neanderthals. No, no, that's not even good enough for those guys. Piltdown men. Yeah, that's what they are. Not real men by any stretch of the imagination."

It absolutely did help to talk out loud to herself as she chipped away at the ice, working her way toward a huge dark blob. This was the biggest deposit they'd discovered yet. So of course, Professor McFayden decided only a sample from this discovery would do.

Not one a mile closer to camp, not even one five miles closer to camp. It had to be this one.

"He wants a sample? I'll show him a sample. Of my fist." Except she wouldn't. She hated conflict, and it showed. Each day her soft soul was more black and blue and purple with bruises from the constant jabs. But she didn't see any way out. This was her final semester before she had to defend her dissertation, and without McFayden's support, she wouldn't graduate. He held all the power.

"Respected advisor and trailblazing scientist, my chubby butt." She gave the ice pick a good hard swing and the teensiest, tiniest bit of ice flew off.

She'd been hacking at the ice for the last thirty minutes, and barely made a dent. At this rate, she really would die of hypothermia before she got that sample she needed.

Genny leaned her forehead against the stupid ice, closed her eyes, and wrapped her gloved hand around the magenta-colored carved stone necklace her parents had sent her a few weeks ago when she'd expressed her worry about coming on this trip. Her mom very readily accepted supernatural, paranormal, occult, or pseudo-scientific phenomena, or emotion-based beliefs and explanations as a natural part of everyday life.

She didn't believe in that kind of woo-woo like her mom, but she acknowledged that there was neuroscience that could explain how meditation changed brain chemistry. Right now, she needed a minute, or she was actually going to give up.

She wasn't going to cry. She was going to breathe. Deep, and slow, and calming.

One breath in, one breath out. Think of the ocean, warm water lapping at her toes. She could do this. Everything would be fine as soon as this trip was over, and she'd graduated.

Drips of wet hit her cheeks and dribbled down her face. Dammit. She'd said she wouldn't cry.

But... she wiped her face. These weren't her tears, and at this temperature, they would have frozen into little beads of ice bedazzling her eyelashes and cheeks.

She opened her eyes and lifted her forehead from the wall of ice. In the spot where her mouth and nose had been, there was now a huge hole in the ice face. It was melting, drips of water pouring down like a leaky faucet. Not from her breath. Couldn't be.

The black splodgy stuff then? But why? Her brain went into hypothesis mode. Had there been some of the unknown substance near the surface and it reacted to the gases in her exhalation? She breathed on the surface again, and the rate of melt increased substantially.

Chunks of the ice crumbled off like a refrigerator with an icemaker dropping its load. Better not try and replicate that occurrence. She stepped back and grabbed her pack to get out her notebook and begin recording these findings.

As she turned, something inside the melted hole flashed and caught her eye. A purple glow came from within. More chemical reactions? That was the only thing she could think of off the top of her head that might cause a luminescence like that.

Was the black substance biological and not some kind of mineral as she'd originally presumed? Could this be bioluminescence in reaction to the warmth or the oxygen or even the carbon dioxide? If so, this wasn't her field but at the same time, it was fascinating.

She leaned in to peer closer at the spot that glowed. The light grew brighter and was concentrated in one particular area that formed a rectangular, almost crystalline shape. That wasn't biological. That was pure geology.

And not anything she'd studied. Had she discovered a new mineral? That glowed purple? If so, she would get to name it. How exciting. She could be really vain and call it Magentonium or... not. There was no way she'd get to even claim the find except as a footnote that she'd been on the expedition once McFayden found out. Then it would have to be called McFuck-ertonium.

The ice was rapidly melting and if she had just a little patience, she'd be able to get to both the black deposits and the crystal. She couldn't help but be anxious and maybe accidentally on purpose blew on the ice again to see if it would melt even faster.

It did. Boy oh boy, did it. In a matter of seconds, she could see the whole crystal and more. So. Much. More. The crystal wasn't some random chunk of mineral stuck in the ice. Nope. It was attached to a black cord, that was sitting on... a chest.

A man's chest.

Her heart went totally arrhythmic, skipping every other beat, then pounding hard to catch back up.

This was no geological discovery. This was going to be the anthropological finding of the millennium. She'd discovered an ice man. Fully intact, preserved perfectly in the ice. She couldn't yet see his facial features, but his clothes were some kind of homespun and leather, and when she thought about it for a second, didn't actually look all that warm.

She stood up, walked away, walked back, looked in the hole again, bit her lip, and shook her hands to work out some of the energy flowing through her like electricity.

A man. In the ice. In Antarctica.

People didn't live here. Maybe she'd discovered a fellow scientist who'd come here and died while exploring. That happened. Right?

No. There was something entirely different about the man frozen in ice and time. She felt... this was ridiculous, but she felt like she knew him. Knew who this was.

She peered into the hole again and blew on the ice in a long swirling breath like she was blowing out the candles on her birthday cake. Screw the science. She needed to see this man's face.

Right now. Like, right the fuck now.

Genny threw off her gloves, and clawed at the ice around the hole, yanking on it with all her might. A chunk the size of a big dog fell and tumbled to the side. It should have squashed her. It was almost as if that ice looked at her and said, "Oh, excuse me, I'll just go over here instead." Which was weird because ice clearly wasn't sentient.

Oh, geez. She must already be suffering from hypothermia because she was clearly losing her mind. Even more strangely, she didn't care. She absolutely had to get to this man in the ice, and it didn't matter if she was crazy, or hypothermic, or throwing her career down the drain by not carefully recording everything for scientific posterity.

The closer she got, the easier the ice fell away or melted under her touch, almost like magic, and the brighter that purple crystal he was wearing around his neck glowed. If she could just touch it, touch him, she would feel... better? No that wasn't right. Feel whole? No, that really was crazy.

Didn't matter. She was getting to her ice man. Yeah. He was hers, goddammit. Professor McFayden would one-thousand-percent try to horn in on this discovery, just like she knew he would on the black deposits. This time, she wasn't going to stand for it. He could go fuck himself. She was claiming this man... uh, discovery for herself.

Another few more chunks fell away and before she could even comprehend what she'd accomplished in moving a sheer wall of ice, she was standing before the most handsome man she'd ever seen in her life. Too bad he was dead. Like a few hundred or thousand years dead.

She always did go for the unavailable guys.

"What are you doing here, ice man of mine?" The question came out whispered. It wasn't as if anyone could hear, but it felt right to talk to him anyway. She reached up and placed her palm on his cheek, needing to touch him.

The world went supernova. His necklace flashed blue and purple light so bright, she should have been blinded. Ice man's eyes slowly opened, and he blinked down at her. "I'm looking for demon wyrms."

He smacked his tongue in his mouth a few times, like the words tasted strange coming out of his mouth. "What are you doing here, my sweet blue witch?"

Genny jumped about a foot in the air and fell right onto her butt in the pile of slushy ice. "What? How? Who?"

The man wriggled his shoulders, then his hips, and pulled himself out of the rest of the ice, stomping his feet. His bare feet?

Once Genny re-kickstarted her brain she got up and took a good safe step back. "How... how are you alive? You were frozen in the ice for who knows how long."

He stretched his arms and twisted his torso one way and then the other, as if just waking up from a nap. "Was I? Those damn little demons. A Dragon Warrior is not so easily killed."

Dragon warrior? That must be his clan or tribe, his people. If he was from another time and presumably not modern-day America, not with that outfit, how did he speak English so easily?

"Thank you for freeing me. Are you also here to hunt the little beasties? I welcome the company and assistance from a powerful witch like yourself." He closed the space between them and pulled her into his arms. "Shall we mate now, or would you prefer to find shelter first?"

Whoa, whoa, whoa. "Mate? I think we're having a difference in culture and - or communication. Just because I discovered you in the ice and got you free, does not mean we're going to... have sex."

"Ah, you would prefer I woo you first. I assure you I am excellent in the art of bed sport. You will not want for orgasms."

She should be horrified right now. So, uh, why wasn't she? Why did his cocksureness turn her on when every other man she'd been around for the past few years made her feel utterly disgusting if they acted anything like this guy right now?

"Oh, umm. Thanks? But I don't think that would be appropriate."

"Giving my mate orgasms is always appropriate."

Okay. She understood now. He'd woken up out of a deep cryogenic sleep, which was a scientific discovery all on its own, but with some kind of disassociation or dementia. He thought she was his wife or something.

"I think you're confused. I am not your mate."

"Of course you are. Look at how my soul shard glows for you." He lifted the crystal on the cord around his neck and held it between their faces. The purple light from within pulsed just like a heartbeat. "Although, it seems to have changed colors. Regardless, it clearly indicates you are my fated mate. I'm happy to have found you."

Genny slowly extricated herself from ice man's arms and pointed toward her snowmobile. "Why don't we get you back to the camp and you can explain what a soul shard is, how you got stuck in the ice, and where... or when you're from."

Fated mate. Yeah, right.

Wouldn't that be nice.

SNOUTLANDER

*P*orfirio could not keep his eyes off his mate. Well, his mate's backside as they raced across the barren snowscape on her magical sleigh. The fates had chosen well. He couldn't have picked better himself.

She was plump and delicious, or he assumed she was under that giant puffy coat she had on. Never had he seen clothing so brightly colored as this or felt such strange material. He'd thought at first that she was a red witch since she was wearing their colors.

There was no doubt she had powerful magic over the element of water just as he did. Not with the way she destroyed the ice, bending it to her will and melting it. Or how the ice and snow parted before her to make a path to her abode. Both spoke of her deep understanding of how to bend the natural world to her will. Even he, as the first son of the first son of the first Blue Dragon Warrior, didn't have as much control as she wielded.

Then there was her sharp, witty mind. The way she spoke was so musical. She spoke a language he'd never heard before, but it reminded him of the Vikings that had brought him to this desolate land of snow and volcanoes. He'd say another prayer of thanks to the First Dragon and the White Witch for imbuing his soul shard with the ability to understand and speak her language.

But he did not like this game of hard to get she was playing. He would woo her properly if she desired, but he'd rather get to the part where he had her writhing on his cock while she came a dozen or more times. Then he could woo her afterwards. They had the rest of their lives to get to know each other.

Besides, with their combined power, no nasty demon wyrms would be able to sneak into the world and wreak their havoc. Just her talent for creating this magnificent sleigh with no horses, reindeer, or dogs to pull it through the snow was a testament to her awesome magic. She must have power over more than one element to be able to create such a thing.

Why was she here where Ereshkigal and Kur-Jara's

demon wyrms had found a way out of Hell? Did she and her people live here? Or was she already fighting alongside him and his brethren in the war against the Chaos?

He had many questions to ask her, and then he would mark her, claim her, mate her, and give her a hundred orgasms. But then they needed to cross the ocean so he could report back to his Wyr on what he'd found. The Blue Dragon Warriors would be best suited to destroy this particular portal to Hell, even if the Reds thought they were the only ones who could battle the forces of evil.

Her sleigh sped across the snow almost as fast as he could have flown them. Soon he saw the small circle of huts where her people must live. They were strange buildings, not made of stone, wood, or any other material he recognized. There wasn't even smoke billowing out of chimneys. How strange.

She pulled the sleigh up beside one of the larger buildings and they dismounted. She looked him up and down, and he straightened his spine, wanting to look every bit the warrior he was under her perusal. "You can't go in there looking like you just walked off the set of Game of Thrones beach vacay. Here, put on my coat. Hopefully, no one will notice I'm not wearing it.

They probably won't. These guys don't give to two shits about me."

He did not like her words nor her scent when she spoke of these 'guys'. She smelled of a bitter orange, but it wasn't exactly fear, more like unhappiness and resignation. "I will eat them if you'd like. I am quite hungry."

His mate made a very adorable snorting laugh sound. He would enjoy making her laugh. "Uh, thanks for the offer. I may take you up on it later. But listen. I don't want them or anyone to know who or what you are until I can get you back to the States, so when we go in here, I think you should pretend to be my boyfriend."

"I am not a boy and while I will be your friend for all of eternity, we are much more than that."

"Right, the mate thing. Boyfriend kind of means the same thing to my people." She pushed the coat toward him, and he struggled to fit his arms in. The back of the garment stretched to span his shoulders, but it would not close. "So, can you pretend that we've been mates for a while, and you've come to visit me? Then we can go hide in my room, which is going to be awfully tight quarters, and I'll figure out how to get us out of here as soon as possible."

He had many thoughts on how fate worked and whether they had been mates since the beginning of time, but that was for a later discussion. What she wanted from him now was a ploy so she could avoid the 'guys.' He would rather eat them, but he would do as she wished.

Guys must mean men. He did not like that she lived with men, but perhaps they offered her protection in exchange for her magic. That had better be all they asked of her. He knew she had not formed any other type of bonds with them because she neither smelled of any other male scents, nor did she show any signs of affection for them. Otherwise, he would have to eat each and every one of them.

"I agree to participate in your hoax if it means I get to spend more time with you and not the men causing you irritation. Although, I don't know why you don't use your powers to either freeze them or drown one of them. That would teach the others a lesson not to bother you."

"Shit, your feet. How do you not have frostbite? Umm, tell them your boots got ruined and—"

Porfirio cupped his mate's chin and brushed his lips across hers to lend her his strength. "My sweet flower, allow yourself to be calm. Your mind is a wonder, but you cannot solve every scenario before we even walk into battle. I trust in your wit to get us through whatever situation we may face. And if it all goes awry, I will shift and fly us to the ocean."

Her cheeks went a beautiful pink with warmth. He could hardly wait to make the rest of her skin from her toes up do the same thing once he had her naked.

"I... okay. You're right, I can't solve every potential problem before we walk in there, and we can't stand out here any longer or we'll freeze to death." She put her hands over her mouth and made a surprised face. "Sorry, I didn't mean, but you know, you didn't freeze to death, you were just—"

He pressed a finger to her lips, turned her around to face the entrance to the building and gave her a small shove toward the door. The sooner he got this meeting with the men she lived with over, the sooner he could get her into bed and complete their mating.

That one swift taste of her lips wasn't near enough.

They pushed open the door and were met first with an outer chamber where many coats and other strange winterwear hung from hooks. They could hear music and talking coming from inside. One loud and arrogant voice in particular filtered through the next doorway.

"Seriously, what kind of name is Magenta? Probably the color of her pussy. Bet it's turned blue out there on that wild goose chase I sent her on. It's not like it can get any more frozen than it is." The statement was followed by a few hearty laughs, but a few more that sounded forced.

"Oh dear seven-pound baby Jesus." She looked up at him with embarrassment in her eyes. He was definitely murdering whoever said such vile things. They weren't worthy of being his snack. What he hated even more was that she thought she needed to cover for them. "I'm sorry to subject you to such asshattery. They're... a lot."

"They are nothing. Less than. Soon you will never need to hear nor see them ever again. That I promise you." If she was here for these people's protection, she no longer needed it as he would protect her now. She was his, and he would never let anyone hurt her with words or weapon ever again.

Her lips and forehead pushed into a frown, but as he stared down at her, willing her to feel the sincerity in his words, they slowly turned to a tentative smile. "Then let's do this."

She pushed open the inner door, and they entered into what he decided was their version of a pub. He did not see a minstrel, but music filled the small building, as did a group of men, all drinking from ale horns. They all stopped mid-sentence and turned as one to gawk at the two of them.

His mate raised one hand in a half wave. "Uh, hi. This is my boyfriend, uh..."

She looked up at him with panic in her eyes. She didn't know his name, and if he supplied it to her the men would catch them in the ruse.

An all too familiar jovial voice boomed across the room. "Porfirio, my boy, where the Hell have you been? We've been waiting on you."

A tall and wizened warrior, with only one arm and a smile that lit up the room, waved him and his mate over. He'd turned some wooden crates into a makeshift bar and was serving up the horns of ale from behind it. Porfirio stared at the man, feeling nothing but faith and trust in him. He did not belong here, and yet, Porfirio had no idea who he was or why he felt that way.

His mate took the cue and quickly crossed to the bar, putting as much space between them and the men who must be the fabled 'guys.'

A woman, almost as beautiful as his mate appeared from behind the barkeep. She was dressed in a flowing white gown and looked as though she was the embodiment of the sun, wind, earth, fire, and water all rolled into one. He wanted to bow before her.

The woman in white waved his mate over and embraced her in a warm and welcome hug. "There's our Magenta. We've been waiting on you too. I'm so happy to see you two found each other. It took me a long time to find the just the right one for our lost little lamb. Come. I've made you a nice hot toddy."

The arrogant man sauntered over to the bar and pushed his ale horn to the barkeep. "Ina, Kur, you know my grad student, Genny?"

The woman ignored the man completely, but the barkeep refilled the horn and handed it back, sloshing some of the contents onto the man's hands. "Of course. Porfirio is part of our team, and the two of them have been together for what seems like forever. We can hardly wait for them to get hitched."

Arrogant man turned on Porfirio and gave him a measuring look. "What's your field, Pinocchio?"

"He studies the atmosphere trapped in the ice from the, uh... I forget which period." Magenta, Genny, he liked her name, intervened before Porfirio could freeze or drown this piece of shit.

The barkeep filled in the missing information. But he looked directly at Genny as he said it. "Tenth century. Our Porfirio is a tenth century... person."

Arrogant man took a swig from his ale. "Two questions, Pinocchio. What the fuck is in the tenth century worth studying, and how the fuck did you hook up with our round, little Gen Gen? Oh, wait, one more question. She's a good lay, isn't she? The more the cushion, the better the pushing. Am I right?"

Genny gasped. "Professor McFayden, that's so inappropriate."

There was no room to shift in this small space, or this McFayden man would already be in Porfirio's belly. He didn't want to destroy the shelter the other humans and his witch resided in, but he did have every need to end this man and his arrogance.

He brought his fist back and put all the power he had into the punch. A second before his punch met the McFayden's face, the barkeep caught his fist in his and held it firm. Porfirio couldn't budge. The barkeep was no mere mortal.

In a low and firm voice meant only for Porfirio's ears, the barkeep gave his advice. "This tainted human will not remember any of this tomorrow. My luscious and clever mate has taken care of that. But this wyrm in human's clothing would wake up and wonder why he no longer has an eyeball in that socket if I allow you to give him what he deserves in this moment."

That sounded fine and dandy to him. "I will destroy him. It's now or later."

"Later." The barkeep gave a small shake of his head. "Remember your mission, son."

A warmth he hadn't known he was missing seeped

into Porfirio at the barkeep's words. His mission. Seek out and destroy the wyrms who have escaped in the frozen south. The immortal was telling him McFayden was a clue to how or why the wyrms had been escaping through this portal and what they were doing among the humans.

Porfirio dropped his arm and used it for something much more fun. He wrapped it around his mate. "Let's go, my Genny. You need not be in the presence of such filth any longer than necessary."

She leaned into him and took long deep breaths against his chest, calming herself, just as much as him. "My room is this way."

"Hey, kid." The warrior barkeep called to him. "Take my advice and give your mate lots and lots of orgasms. They like that."

The woman in white smacked the warrior with a wet towel that snapped, but she grinned as she did.

That was an order he could follow.

A PURPLE PASSION

Something well beyond the complex explanations of science was going on here. Genny's well-ordered life, as miserable as it was, just went flipped, turned upside down.

Sure, she'd seen McFayden drink till he was messy before, but he'd been out of his friggin skull back there. And who exactly were those people serving up the drinks? The woman in white should have been shivering her butt off in nothing but that flowy dress, yet she'd seemed cozy and warm as a cup of hot chocolate.

"You are taking me to your private rooms?" her iceman asked, with plenty of lusty suggestion in his voice.

"Room. Just one. And it's awfully small and going to be very cramped with the two of us in there until morning." What the hell was she thinking bringing a strange man to her bedroom. The rumors about her we're going to fly tomorrow. And you know what? For the first time since she'd been admitted to the state university's PhD program, she didn't care what the guys thought or said about her. They weren't the ones who had made the discovery of the millennium.

"We'll need to hide out there until morning, when I can figure out how to get you back to the mainland." Although it wasn't like she knew what she was going to do after that. It wasn't like ages old ice men had passports. She had no idea how she was going to get him from Australia, the closest continent to Antarctica, all the way back to the U.S.

They couldn't exactly take a commercial flight, and she didn't have the kind of funds to find him black market papers anyway. What the hell was she thinking? She didn't have a plan, and even if she did, it was doomed to fail. She really ought to march back out there and present her iceman to the rest of the scientists.

No matter how much she knew that was the right thing to do, she absolutely could not. Even thinking about it made the inside of her chest go colder than ice. This man was hers. Which was a really weird thing to think. She didn't own him, she didn't even know what to do with him.

"There is no morning nor night in this land. But I will happily spend many hours in your bed with you, until we fly away from this frozen continent." He pulled Genny close and wrapped her into his arms. With a sexy low growl, he buried his face in the crook of her neck and she forgot how to breathe.

Wait, did he say fly? He wasn't supposed to know about airplanes. "Hold up there, mister. As much as I am enjoying your attention, I think you need to tell me what is going on here."

She pulled away but grabbed his hand and tugged him down the narrow hallway, and into the tiny room where she slept and worked on her research. She may not have a lot of privacy in this small research center, but in her own room with the door shut and locked, no one would disturb them.

Genny wasn't wrong when she thought that it would be cramped with the two of them in here. He was approximately the size of a Viking crossed with an NFL linebacker crossed with Mr. Universe, and she was no small fry. She glanced down at the single cot. Most nights the bars along the edge of her bed poked into her hips, thighs, and butt. It was not gear made for a plus size woman. This was going to be one cramped night. Unless, of course, she snuggled up into his arms.

Whoa, whoa, whoa. That thought was completely inappropriate. Sure, he was sex on a stick. A sexy popsicle. She almost snort laughed at her own thought but caught herself. Just because he was flirty didn't mean a thing. Perhaps that was just the everyday culture of his people. She would not take advantage of the fact that he was a fish out of water in her place and time. No matter how much she actually wanted to kiss him. Bad scientist, bad, bad, scientist.

He looked around her room with a frown. "You must be a powerful witch to wield the elements to do your bidding like this. Do you have control of all four?"

OK, so that confirmed he was from a time where magic and witchcraft was an important part of society. But that didn't exactly narrow it down, except to somewhere before the last three-hundred years or so. It also ruled out the possibility that he was a more modern explorer who'd been trapped in the ice. "When and where exactly are you from?"

That was a stupid question. He didn't even yet know that he wasn't still in that time and place. She had so many more pressing things to ask him. Like how did he speak English and why wasn't he dead?

She couldn't seem to stay in her logical mind when

she was around him. "Sorry, forget I said that. Let's start at the beginning. What is your name and where are you from?"

Her iceman ran his thumb along her cheek and down her jawline, while looking so deeply into her eyes that she thought he might fall into her. Or perhaps she was the one falling.

She ought to turn the heat down, it was getting stupidly hot in here. She unzipped the fleece vest she had been wearing underneath her jacket. Her iceman followed suit and shed her big puffy coat and dropped it onto the bed.

"I am Porfirio Kahurangi, heir to the Blue Dragon Wyvern. I live in and around an island not far from here, as the currents flow. Tell me your name, sweet flower." He didn't stop with the jacket, also shedding the homespun style shirt he was wearing too.

Holy six pack abs. Ack. Sweet baby Jesus in the manger, what was her name?

Concentrate, concentrate. What did he just say?

An island not far from here? The closest land was Australia. She guessed it was sort of a big island. "I'm Genny, short for Magenta. Do you know where we are now?"

"Magenta. Delicious. I do know where we are." He stepped closer to her, not that he had far to go, and took up all the space and air in the room. "My father sent me to this island of ice to investigate the demons swarming from the volcano. The question is, my lovely mate, what are you doing here? Humans, even witches as powerful as you, don't live long in this frozen land."

Not frozen. Hot. So, so hot.

Oh, right. Antarctica was frozen. Right. And she supposed central heat, modern materials, and electronics would look like magic to someone who lived before the industrial age.

"I'm also here to study the volcano." She didn't want to say much more than that. She'd already contaminated his knowledge when she shouldn't have. Why did he refer to her as a human? Strange.

Porfirio reached for the zipper on her lighter-weight jacket she wore under her other outerwear. He eyeballed the metal slider, then gave it a small tug. His eyes lit up with that same pretty purple glow that his amulet had as he pulled the zip down, revealing her long sleeved t-shirt, necklace, and bit of skin at the nape of her neckline. "Did your coven also note the demon activity here? Do you fight against Ereshkigal's forces of evil as we Dragon Warriors do?"

She really should've studied anthropology. Talking to this man about his culture was way more interesting than trying to talk to rocks. Although, rocks didn't make her feel flutters in her tummy or get warm and squirmy between the legs either. "Who is Air-ish-kegel?"

"The Queen of the Underworld. She and her consort, Nergal, the God of Chaos, wreak havoc on our world. The Dragon Warriors' duty is to keep humanity safe from their demons." As he said these words, he skimmed his knuckles across her color bone, sending a sensation of pleasure through her so great that she had to clench the muscles between her legs.

"I have waited hundreds of years to find you, my luscious mate. Let me mark you, claim you for my own, and make you my one true mate now. I promise to give you many orgasms and keep you safe forever-more." He wrapped his hand around the purple stone on the chain her parents had sent and a whoosh of... well she didn't know what it was, shuddered the entire room.

Her necklace disintegrated in his hand and a tornado of colorful fragments—red, orange, yellow, green, blue, and purple swirled around them. Porfirio's own amulet went supernova and filled her small quarters with the most brilliant bright purple light.

He grabbed her around the waist and lifted her up, so she had to wrap her legs around his waist. "Ah, you see, the White Witch and the First Dragon have blessed our union. You cannot deny now that we are meant to be mates forevermore."

He may be from Australia, but she knew better than to think that mates meant friends. A union. With the ancient man she'd dug out the ice. That should scare her to no end. All the men in her life, except her dad, were absolute trashy pigs.

Just thinking about taking him up on his offer wasn't even close to logical. But she wanted it. More than anything.

"What does that mean, to mark?" Like, was he going to tattoo her? She didn't do great with pain.

"Let me show you, sweet Magenta." His words were a soft growl, and he lowered his lips to the exposed skin at her throat.

The way he said her name had her knees going weak. Okay, if this marking came with kisses too, she could handle some needles, or whatever instruments ancient ice men used. Later, she'd introduce him to antibiotics just for funsies.

Porfirio pressed his lips to a sensitive spot just under her ear and then nibbled his way down the column of her throat. Why, oh why, was she wearing so many layers right now?

"You have on entirely too many clothes," he whispered into her ear as if he'd been reading her thoughts.

His fingers skimmed the hemline of her t-shirt, and he reached his fingers underneath, grazing the side of her stomach with his knuckles. "Let me help you off with them so I can mark you properly."

Ugh, under the shirt she also had on a tank top and silk thermals. She didn't even know why. It wasn't like she was cold. In fact, she hadn't felt even the slightest bit chilly since that first breath of hers had started melting the ice.

"Yes, please, right now. Take it off. Take everything off." Genny hadn't even waited for him to strip her shirt over her head. That probably would have been sexier, but did she care right now? Nope. She just wanted to be naked with this man, who she also wanted to be naked. As soon as possible.

In one fell swoop, she was standing in front of him with nothing on from the waist up but her very sensible, yet colorful, bra.

Porfirio's eyes wandered all along her curves, glowing brighter with every turn. In the past she might have crossed her arms to hide her belly and stretch marks. But the way that he was looking at her, she felt more like flaunting her body before him.

He licked his lips. "I do believe that purple is my new favorite color."

The way the purple light both from behind his eyes

and from the amulet he wore pulsed as he said that, it was hers now too. The way her body was going warm and fuzzy from the inside out, how her heart beat so hard she could actually feel it in her chest, and the feel-good sparklies firing in her neurons had an absolute and complete hold on her.

Whatever was happening between her and Porfirio couldn't be explained by science. This was pure magic.

"I don't understand what's happening, but I know somewhere deep inside, it's right." She pressed her hands to his broad, bare chest, needing the connection. "Do you feel it too?"

"I've seen others find their true mates, but I had no idea how powerful I would feel once I found you. I promise I'll explain anything and everything you want to know, but after I've marked, claimed, and mated you, my sweet gem." He lowered his lips again, and this time went straight for the crook of her neck. He licked over her collar bone and kissed a particularly sensitive spot. Her knees did buckle this time.

But Porfirio's arms were there to catch her. He picked her up and laid her on the cot, crawling over her, never once letting his lips leave her skin.

Genny wrapped an arm around his shoulders and threaded the other into his hair, wanting to hold him to her, never letting him go. The cot creaked under them, and she didn't care even a little bit if it collapsed under their combined weight.

No man had ever kissed her or touched her like this before. She'd had the occasional snogging session with guys at parties during her undergrad years, but she hadn't been with anyone since she started grad school. Porfirio's touch proved to her exactly how much she'd missed out on.

Not that any other man would do. It was his touch that she longed for, even before she even knew he existed.

He opened his mouth and scraped his teeth across her skin. Genny moaned so loud that there was no way the rest of the crew on this mission didn't hear her.

And she didn't care. "Do that again, please."

"I'll do you even better." He licked that same spot and this time instead of a scrape of the teeth, he sank his teeth into her skin, biting her, sucking her flesh into his mouth.

Stars exploded, volcanoes erupted, and the world shook, as she came harder than she ever had in her entire life. All from a simple bite.

In her mind, she heard Porfirio's voice, on a long, low growl, saying the word, "Mine."

She wanted to scream that she was his, but she was too busy writing in ecstasy as her body pulsed and rode out her orgasm as if she'd never stop coming.

Bang. Bang. Bang. Someone was pounding on the door to her room. "Genny, shut up, you whore."

Before she couldn't even fathom a response, Porfirio was up and off of her in a flash. He ripped the door right off its hinges and grabbed Professor McFayden up by his throat. "You'll apologize to my mate, and then I'll squash you like a demon wyrm."

Oh shit. She definitely wasn't going to graduate now.

But did she actually care? Maybe not if more orgasms like that were in her future.

NO SUCH THING AS PURPLE DRAGONS

*P*orfirio wanted nothing more than to mark and claim his mate so that they could start the rest of their lives together. But first he had to destroy this human piece of garbage who dared to insult his Genny.

There simply wasn't enough space in this tiny room, or even the building, to shift into his dragon form, so he would have to be more creative with his murder tactics. Otherwise, he would have just eaten the man in one giant bite.

Calling upon his skills and training as a warrior, he spun and kicked the door open. That move did exactly as he hoped and sent the piece of shit flying back to smack into a spiky wall of ice opposite Genny's room.

Porfirio watched with a satisfied glee as the asshole slumped against the ice, dazed and confused.

"Oh no, Porfirio." Genny jumped up and wrapped the blanket around her luscious body. Too bad. Another thing this horrible man had wrought. If he had his druthers, his mate would be naked all the time. But he would also like to hide her away in his hoard, which meant they could not fight demons together. Choices, choices.

She peeked around him and stared down at the limp pile of human on the floor, tiny icicles and drips of melted ice water dripping onto his head. "I both love that you did that and have to ask you to stop before you beat up my advisor."

Genny grabbed him by the elbow and hid herself behind him, as if she was still afraid of this man when he was unconscious. What else had he done to her to make her feel so afraid of him? She clearly had the power to protect herself from him. Porfirio would find out and then mete out punishment as was deserving.

"This despicable excuse for a man gives you advice? You should expel him from your coven and your life immediately. He is unworthy of your presence. He does not deserve to be seen or heard by any woman if he speaks of them with such disdain." He gave the man a long sniff. It was meant with derision, but with that whiff, the odor of evil wafted through Porfirio's senses.

Genny fidgeted and peeked at her former advisor again before stepping back into her room and pacing. "No, well, yes, he does give me advice, but on my education. Without his approval I can't graduate. God, I hope he's too drunk to remember any of this. Or I am so screwed."

"Stay back, my gem. Your advisor is cursed with the taint of chaos." He opened his senses to make sure he hadn't missed other signs of a demon infestation. "I smell it permeating him."

Porfirio squatted down to get a closer look. The man's head lolled to the side, and he groaned but did not open his eyes. A small dribble of black blood oozed from his nose. That did not look like blood. It more resembled the oily stain of the remains of a demon wyrm.

Good thing he hadn't tried to eat the man. Whatever had possessed or poisoned this man's soul would not have tasted good at all.

"I refuse to allow this thing in your presence for another moment. We are leaving this icy land. I shall take you back to my home and we will complete our mating there. Then you can meet the rest of my Wyr." He turned his back on the doomed man. It wouldn't be long before the poison of the underworld consumed his soul. A fitting end for a piece of shit.

The distress on his mate's face hurt him right in the center of his chest. "Do not worry, mate. I will never let anyone hurt you ever again."

Especially not someone demon-possessed and touched by chaos. He didn't like that the forces of evil might have been interested in his precious mate in the first place. It had to be why fate had sent him to this land of ice and snow. Those clever masters of the universe knew his mate would need protecting as they fought the demon plague side by side.

She looked up at him and a longing shuddered through her eyes but was gone in a flash. If he hadn't been paying attention, he might have missed it. This need buried deep inside that she tried so hard to hide wasn't the lusty kind.

"There is very little I have dreamed about more than the day I get to leave this ice hole." She waved her arms around indicating the shelter they currently occupied. "We can't go anywhere until I can arrange for transportation. But I do not want to bear the brunt of the fall out tomorrow morning."

She shook her head, looking as if she was lost.

He would drown the world and freeze it over to give her what she wanted and make her happy. He never wanted to see this look on her face again. Hidden in those eyes was the longing for love, attention, affection, and someone to put her and her needs first. He recognized that in her because he felt the same.

Dragon Warriors served, they protected, they sacrificed to keep the world safe, and their one reward was knowing they had a fated mate, their one true love, the one person who would complete their soul with their love.

But in recent years, not all Dragon Warriors had been able to find their mates. Many found companions, but their soul shards, the gift from the mother of all dragons to her people, didn't light up. The connections either lost or never found.

It was why he was on this mission in the first place. Chaos was seeping into the world in places he should not, sneaking, spying, and spreading his special brand of stealthy destruction among humans and supernaturals alike.

Of course the humans didn't understand the ways of the old gods and goddesses. They used their new one-god as a weapon to hunt witches, wolves, dragons, and all manner of paranormal beings.

The wolves had retreated into their own society, banning their people from mating with humans so they could hide in peace. The witches were literally being burned at the stake. The Dragon Warriors no longer flew through the skies or swam the waters openly, although they continued to fight against the evil.

Already humans were beginning to forget they weren't the only intelligent beings on this planet, and their very own neighbors were relegated to folk tales and bedtime stories. If this was how humans treated their women, then they didn't deserve them anyway. He knew plenty of dragon warriors who would happily take a luscious lady off of any human male's hands.

Porfirio grabbed the layers of clothes he just stripped off his mate and her big fluffy coat and handed them to her. "You do not need to arrange anything. I will take care of getting us back to my home."

Now to determine whether they could swim, or if he had to fly. Since he was a blue water dragon that would be the fastest, but even though he had seen her power over the water element, not all humans or even witches used it the same as dragons. She may not be able to be underwater for as long as the swim would take them.

"What do you mean you'll take care of it? You've

been frozen in ice for hundreds of years." As soon as the words came out of her mouth, she slapped her hands over her lips. "Oops. Pretend I didn't say that."

Hundreds of years? No. "You are mistaken, I'm sure. I eviscerated the demon wyrms a mere few hours ago."

Genny's eyebrows shot up her forehead, and her eyes went as round as the moon. "Oh. Yes. That's what I meant to say. I was just being silly, exaggerating."

Hmm. He'd believe her except she would no longer look at him and instead busied herself with putting her clothes back on. Which was a shame, because he hadn't yet gotten to see his mark form on her skin where he had bitten her and shared part of his soul with hers. They would talk more about whatever it was she was hiding from him, but later, when he had her secure and safe in his home and among his hoard.

As soon as she was re-dressed, Porfirio took Genny's hand and lead her back towards the area where they'd met the friendly barkeep and his mate. Perhaps they would also like to return to a warmer climate and friendlier company. Besides, he had a feeling they would have information about whatever was going on with the demons and this barren icy land. As of now, he had nothing to report back to his father aside from finding far too many of the wyrms crawling out of the volcanoes here.

But when they reached the bar, there was only one lonely patron, and all the joviality from before had died away. The remaining man sat doing some sort of magic, punching his fingers rhythmically in front of a glowing book laid on its side. "My gem, I hate to interrupt one of your fellows while he is spellcasting, but I would like to leave a message for the barkeep before we leave. Is it safe to speak to him?"

Genny glanced at the male witch and frowned. "You mean that guy? He's not, umm, doing any real magic at the moment. I think it's fine to talk to him. But maybe tell me the message, and I will approach him, just in case."

Ah, his brave little mate, protecting him just as he would her. Perhaps the man was only studying the glowing grimoire. She had mentioned something about doing studies with her horrible advisor.

"Yes, please. Ask him to tell the barkeep and his mate that I invite them to visit the Blue Dragon Wyr in the Land of the Long White Cloud, if they so like. We would be happy to have them."

"Long white cloud? Is that where you want to take me? That's your home?"

"It is. Aotearoa is lush and even in winter, much more hospitable than this place. You will love the beaches and beautiful land."

"Ow tay-uh row-uh? Oh. Ohh." Her face lit up, excitement flashing through her. "New Zealand. You're from New Zealand. Of course, it's not called that to you, pretend I didn't say that."

New Zee Land. What a strange name for his island. But of course, not all people from around the world called places by the same name. After they returned to deliver the news to his father, the Blue Dragon Wyvern, about the little beasties here, they could venture to her homeland too. He would love to meet her people as well.

Eventually they would call Aotearoa home, once he became the Wyvern. He supposed it was his right as the leader of his Wyr, to relocate if he so chose. The Blue Dragons had only recently relocated to the lush paradise of the Land of the White Cloud along with the islanders they watched over who were explorers of the sea and always looking for a new place to call home.

Genny conferred with the male witch and wrote something down for him as well. How smart and learned his witch was. Few humans could read or write, and the pride swelled in him that his mate was such a rare jewel. His people would be happy to someday call her Wyvern by his side.

He relished the day the White Witch hid his mate's

ring, setting the trail for her to prove she was his true mate, a mate worthy of becoming a leader and mother to the future Wyvern heir. She was so clever it would take her only mere moments to find it, and how they would celebrate that day.

She returned to him and nodded. "Okay. We're all set. I can hardly believe I'm doing this, and I really, really hope you're not taking me out into the middle of Antarctica to freeze to death."

"I will keep you safe and warm. I promise." Her life and happiness were his main responsibility from this day forward.

"I don't know why, but I one-hundred percent believe you. Let's do this." She raised two fingers to her forehead and saluted him. Then she pitched her voice into a strange monotone. "Take me to your leader."

"My father will be pleased I have found such a powerful mate. Come. I can hardly wait to introduce you to him."

She mumbled something under her breath that he only caught bits and pieces of because of his dragon's astute hearing. Something about this adventure had better not become the ice man cometh.

He agreed that he was done with the cold, and while his power over water included the ability to manipulate ice, he was ready to be back in warmer climes. Together they exited the strange shelter and into the chilly outside air.

Genny headed toward her magical sleigh. "We've already knocked out my advisor, might as well steal a snowmobile too. It's not like I have any more to lose."

"While I did enjoy your magic sleigh ride, love, it will be faster if we swim. Don't worry if you can't breathe under the water, I've considered that, and will bring an air bubble down with us for you."

"Uh. Swim?" She shook her head emphatically. "I'm afraid the ocean is miles from here, not to mention we'd die of hypothermia approximately ten seconds after we hit the water. I may have a little bit of blubber on me, but not enough to keep me warm as a walrus."

"Have you met many walruses? I've found them to be a bit pompous." They never wanted to share their oysters.

"If you prefer, we can fly. At least until we get to warmer waters."

"Crap." Her whole spine sagged. "I was with you until you brought up the flying thing again. I was hoping you thought there was a boat nearby. I'd even kind of hoped for a miracle and that you had some kind of a space-time wormhole hidden around here. But if you're just some kind of eccentric billionaire with a helicopter hidden nearby, I guess I'll take that too."

She stared at him for a moment, her mind at work. "Unless. No, it couldn't be. Maybe. Do you have a spaceship? Are you not from Earth? Oh geez. I went and fell for an alien, didn't I? I hope this is like in the books and you've got some kind of woman pleasing appendages in your pants."

That was the first time he'd seen her genuinely smile. "I assure you, my appendage and I will do everything in our power to please your womanhood."

He brushed a soft kiss over her lips and his dragon roared to life, pushing to get out and take his mate away from this forsaken place. The light from his soul shard burst out into the darkness, throwing purple light across the buildings and snow.

"Ready, my gem?"

She nodded and looked at him with excited anticipation. "More than I've ever been in my life."

Porfirio let the magic of the shift pour through him and, in the next instant, became the great blue beast of his dragon, relishing the feeling of taking up space in the world. He shook his head and straightened his scales.

Something felt slightly off kilter though.

He looked down at Genny who stared at him with

awe and wonder. He preened for her and stretched his wings as far as they could go. Something on his wings caught his attention and he turned his head to stare at his right wing.

His purple wing.

Purple.

His scales weren't the familiar blue anymore.

He was a fucking purple dragon. No dragons were purple. There was no such fucking thing as a purple dragon.

A PURPLE HAZE

*D*ragon.

Big. Ass. Purple. Dragon.

Porfirio wasn't an ice man. He wasn't an eccentric billionaire. He wasn't even a freaking alien.

He was an enormous, fire-breathing, brilliantly sparkling and shiny, purple-ass dragon. Well, actually, she had no idea if he breathed fire. So far all he'd done was stand there and spread out his wings as if showing her how god-damned cool he was.

"Sweet gem," a voice popped into her head, and she gasped. *"Do not be afraid. I'm sure once we get back to Aotearoa all will go back to normal."*

"Holy mind meld. Are you talking in my head? Is this mental telepathy? Do all dragons use telepathy? Are there more dragons? What do you mean back to normal? Is this your natural state of being? I have so many questions!"

He chuckled and his big, scaled chest bounced just as a human's would when they laughed. Now she wished she'd studied biology, or zoology, or cryptozo-ology. Why, oh why, had she picked geology and volcanology? Probably because rocks didn't talk back so they couldn't poke fun at her. People and even animals weren't always so nice.

But now that she had a freaking dragon of her very own, she was going to have him eat all of her enemies, or at least burn them to a crisp.

"While I do love these blood-thirsty tendencies, and I will happily eviscerate anyone you so desire, we will have to ask our friends the Red Dragon Warriors to burn them for you, as I do not breathe fire."

"Was I thinking that out loud? Sorry. I don't actu-ally want you to kill anyone. Just a fun fantasy." Throwing Professor McFuckface into the wall was enough to satisfy her.

She carefully reached out, wanting to touch his scales and see what he felt like. "I'm beginning to understand, I think. You've mentioned your power over the elements a few times and I wasn't putting two and two together, but if red dragons breath fire, do the colors of your scales match the power?

Red for fire, blue for water, green for earth, etcetera?"

"Clever girl. Yes. Gold for wind and sun, and blue for water, like your element."

"But then what's purple?" Electricity? No, he was from a time before people had discovered that. Maybe just lightning? Not that there had been any thunder and lightning storms since she'd melted him out of the ice.

Hmm. What else was purple representative of? Royalty. But that wasn't an element. Maybe she needed to think more like her mother and go a little woo-woo. Spirit?

He lowered his head and touched his snout to her forehead. *"That, my love, is something we will have to figure out together, because up until I met you, I was a Blue Dragon Warrior. Now, I don't even know if I still have power over the element. I'm unsure what I am."*

The vulnerability in his voice tugged at her heart. This was the moment that they understood each other in a way no one else ever could, and she wanted to remember it forever.

He'd also mentioned she had power too. Could she... no. That was silly. "I don't entirely know what I am either, so we'll figure it out together."

"Together, then." He huffed a soft breath of air at her,

and it was filled with snowflakes. Whether that was just because they were in Antarctica or because that's what purple dragons blew instead of fire, she didn't know.

"What do we do now? I don't exactly know how to ride a dragon." Like, did she need a saddle or some kind of harness? Wouldn't she freeze as they flew at high altitudes? Was there enough oxygen for her? Why hadn't she read more *Dragon Riders of Pern* or *How to Train Your Dragon* books instead of National Geographic growing up?

"Calm your mind, mate. All your questions will get answered. I promise."

"Oops. I thought all of that out loud again, didn't I?" She really needed to learn how this mental telepathy worked. She didn't hear all of his thoughts all the time. So, there must be a way to only share what she wanted to. "I'll work on that. No one needs to see all the mess that's inside my head all the time."

"It's not mess. It's you, and I enjoy it." Porfirio spread his wings again, and this time he flapped them and lifted up into the air. Just a couple of feet of the ground, he opened his giant clawed foot and extended it toward her. *"Climb aboard, my lady. You're safe in my hands."*

Eek. He was going to carry her. No one had ever

carried her. Well, not since she was a tubby three-year-old. Then again, no one else she knew was a dragon.

Genny climbed into his claw, and he gently closed the talons around her, creating a secure seat, kind of like one of those fancy egg-chairs. She could see the full three-hundred and sixty degrees around, as he lifted them up into the air.

It had been hard to adjust to a never setting sun when she'd first arrived at the South Pole but getting to see it as she would have from a helicopter or plane, in the eternal light of day, was spectacular. She wished she had a camera.

Instead, she would have to live in the moment and remember this like her own personal snapshot in time. Somehow, she liked that better than recording information to review at a later date. This new feeling was very unscientific, but she kind of liked it.

Porfirio flew much faster than she imagined he would, and it wasn't long before they were approaching the cliffs of the glacier sheet and the ocean. He didn't say anything, but she felt his unease. Genny wrapped her arms around his claw, giving him a sort of awkward hug. The wind was too loud to talk, so she concentrated on sharing her thoughts with him in some kind of coherent speech pattern. *"What's wrong?"*

"The continent of ice looks very different than I remember it from when I flew here only a few days ago. Is this the work of the demon wyrms?"

Oh, crudapalooza. How to explain global warming to a dragon from ancient times? *"I'm afraid that's the dirty business of humans. We haven't been great custodians of the Earth and have caused it to warm up, which has melted the polar ice caps."*

He stayed silent for a while, and Genny didn't push him. They were both discovering a whole new world right now.

"When did the humans do all this? I am concerned the God of Chaos has a hand in a catastrophe such as this."

"You and I have a lot to talk about when we get to your island. Things are not going to be the same for either of us."

"I see that. I am glad we have each other now to lean on in what may be hard times ahead."

Someone to lean on in tough times. That... was so discordant from everything else that had been happening in her life, she almost wanted to cry. The emotions roiled around in her chest along with the whispers from the ugly part of her brain that asked why in the world she deserved such loyalty and dare she say it, love, from a unique and interesting magical man.

If she didn't feel so silly doing it, she'd pinch herself to see if this was all a dream. It had to be, right? Any minute now she was going to wake up and be back in her chilly, bare room in the research center, facing another day of subtle, yet devastating harassment from her peers.

A thick cloud popped up out of nowhere and they were instantly surrounded by the white mist. Genny couldn't see more than a few inches in front of her face, but weirdly, she could see another dragon flying alongside them.

This one was all the colors of the rainbow, had a wonky left wing that looked broken, and had a beautiful woman in a flowing white gown cupped in his claw. Even though the only thing Genny could hear was the whooshing of the air rushing past her ears, when the women opened her mouth to speak, it was as if they were in a quiet room having a cup of tea.

"It's not a dream, Magenta. There's nothing for you to wake up from. Except maybe those false beliefs that have been drummed into your head about being unworthy of the love and gifts that you've been given."

"This sure feels like a dream." Even her mind was filled with fog and mist.

"Oh, that's because this part isn't real at all." The woman in white's voice was like the tinkling of bells.

"You won't even remember it. But I'm here to cultivate those seeds of self-assurance that have been fallow in your mind. I wouldn't have chosen you for such a special Dragon Warrior if I didn't already know exactly how perfect you two are for each other. He'll need your help finding his way in your world."

"Porfirio is amazing." If she could swoon while in a mid-air flight in a dreamworld, she would. "Are you sure I'm good enough for him? It's going to be really hard to introduce him to the twenty-first century."

The rainbow dragon winked at her. "My sons are adaptable. He'll figure it out. and if he doesn't, just tell him to quit being a douchepotato and to give you some more orgasms. Orgasms fix everything."

"Kur." The woman in white rolled her eyes and chastised the dragon, but she also smiled. "Send them on their way now, my love."

The rainbow dragon let his tongue hang out the side of his mouth and then blew a warm breeze in their direction. It sent Porfirio tumbling, spinning through the air like they'd been caught up in a tornado.

He gripped her tighter, closing his talons around her so she didn't tumble out of his grasp even a little. *"Whoa, hold on, sweet gem. We've been hit with a hot air current, and I'm not a Gold Dragon Warrior, so we'll have to ride it out. Don't worry. I've got you."*

"I know. I trust you." And she did. She just hoped that he would also be able to put that same trust in her when they reached land and he saw how different the world was.

It felt like only a few minutes of crossing the bluest of oceans and the light of day turned to night. Far too soon she spotted the lights of civilization on land. That was so fast. She wasn't entirely ready for the real world again.

"Mate, do you know why there are so many fires? Is it a celebration day or has a war among the humans besieged this land?"

Okay, so he probably wasn't an electricity dragon, because if he was, he probably would be able to feel the power of a city blazing with lights. "It's not a war. This is what human cities and towns look like here."

Although, she had no idea where here was. She didn't think it was New Zealand or even Australia. Probably not Africa either. Maybe they'd gone all the way up to India?

As they got closer to the land, things began looking far too familiar. Blinking lights flashed in the sky below them and she realized most of what she thought were stars were actually airplanes. Oh god, what if the government of whatever country they were approaching sent up fighter jets or something? That always happened in the movies. She was going to be pissed if someone tried to shoot her dragon down.

"Porfirio, we should fly down much closer to the water. There are... umm... we aren't alone in the skies, and I'm not sure the others will be flying the friendly skies."

Without even a question, he angled his wings and changed their course exactly as she instructed. He flew them so close to the water, if she reached down, she'd be able to skim her fingers along the gentle waves. *"I have noticed the metal birds gliding along the currents. That blast of wind has taken us to a strange land indeed. I will keep you safe. Do not fear."*

"Right back atcha, big guy." The closer they got to land, the more she knew that vow would be called upon. Because they weren't approaching India, or even Asia, or Europe. This was the East Coast of the United States. She knew because their path was taking them directly toward the Jersey shore, only a few minutes from Rogue, New York. Her hometown.

Well, she hoped Rogue was ready to meet a big purple dragon, because she was bringing one home.

BRIGHT LIGHTS, BIG VILLAGE

*B*oth a peace and anxiety permeated Genny's scent the closer they got to land. He would have thought she would be comfortable over the ocean, seeing as she was a Blue Witch, but perhaps she preferred ice to liquid.

He was glad they were coming in at night, but it was hardly dark. Whatever lights illuminated this human settlement had the power of a thousand tiny suns. He could hardly see the stars in the sky here.

"Head toward that forested area over there. It should be safe. Humans don't go into those woods very often." Her thoughts showed him wolves running through the trees though.

Intriguing. She knew where they were. The supernatural wind that blew them off course brought them to this strange land, and if he was reading her thoughts right, the humans and wolf shifters her lived together.

Midway through their journey, they had crossed the equator, but by the position of the stars, he did not believe they were as far north as to be in the Rus homeland of the wolves. If he had to guess, some of them had rebelled against the Volkov council and joined forces with these humans. That would be a powerful alliance, and he was always down for a bit of rebellion.

To top it all off, the area that Genny guided him to had a large tree in the center in the shape of a dragon. Perhaps some of his brethren were here as well. He'd never heard of a place where dragons, wolves, and humans co-mingled, but perhaps this Wyr knew more of the demon wyrm threat and had chosen to recruit other supernaturals to the fight.

This should be interesting.

He flew in low over a strange town and then toward the dragon tree. Flashes of memories living here flickered through her mind for him to see. Her scent matched the flora, fauna, and salt of the sea here too. Better here than the continent of ice with the horrible advisors she lived with there. *Is this strange land your home?*

But before she could answer, or they could land, a

group of black dragons burst up out of the trees and sent out warning shots of shadow-laced flame at them.

Without conscious though, the instincts of his beast rose up and took over. He tucked Genny tight to his chest and flipped into a backwards loop and spiral to get behind the predators. She screamed as they dove, but he would keep her safe. *"Hold tight, gem, we're in for a battle. If you've got any magic to help, feel free to call upon your spells."*

"What? No, I don't know magic. All I have is pepper spray, which is back in Antarctica, and nine-tenths of a degree in vulcanology." His mate denied her heritage, but even as she spoke, he felt the shift of water molecules in the air.

"I know that you have likely been taught to hide your powers but can be your true self with me. Call upon the elements at your disposal now to fight with me against these demon dragons. An ice wall or your icicles could distract them since they are using some kind of fire."

There was only one black dragon he knew of, and that warrior's soul had been tainted by Ereshkigal in Hell. These must be his offspring, and Porfirio was going to send the whole lot of them back to Hell to meet their maker once again, with the help of his mate.

This was their first battle test together, and he really fucking wished he'd already claimed her and given her his soul. That was at the absolute top of his priority list when they were safe again.

The largest of the black demon dragons opened his wings and hung in the air, shadow swirling around him. He used an alpha voice that was reserved for Wyverns, allowing him to communicate with any other dragon even if they weren't in his Wyr. He pushed his words directly into Porfirio's head. *"Identify yourself, dragon, and yield to my authority. You are in the Black Dragon Brotherhood's territory, and I am the Black Dragon Wyvern."*

"I do not yield, nor accept your authority or claim to this land. There is no Black Dragon Wyr, and thus no Wyvern. You have no command over me or mine. Go back to whence you came." He spun and pulled the breath from within, ready to spew water and ice at the imposter. The magic within bubbled and roiled, ready to defend him and his mate with the power of his element.

When he opened his mouth and called upon the element to breathe his icy stream, only soft flakes of snow spilled forth. Aw, fuck. Whatever spell or curse had been laid upon him to turn him this ridiculous shade of purple had, as he feared, also shuttered his power over water.

The other black dragons surrounded them, covering any route of escape, except down. He flew in a pattern that made it hard for them to aim and spew their fire at him while not hitting the other dragons in the sky, but it wouldn't work for too long. *"It's now or never, sweet gem."*

"Here goes nothing." The scent of her fear and also bravery, sweet as ripe persimmon, filled his senses at the same time as thin, but sharp daggers of ice shot out from under his belly and between his claws.

"Pew, pew, pew." His mate made a sharp pitched sound with each shard of ice she shot at the black dragons.

Unfortunately, the others appeared to be a well-trained unit and easily avoided her attacks. The large black dragon even caught one in his claw and shattered her weapon into a thousand pieces. He said something to the others, that Porfirio could not hear.

As one, they circled him, forcing his flight path to grow smaller and smaller. They were herding him, and in a last-ditch effort, he landed in the highest branches of the dragon tree, grasping on with his free claw, and keeping Genny close to his chest.

"Whoa, I did it. I imagined icicles shooting at them, and that's what happened." She sounded as pleased as if she'd never used her magic before in her whole life. Yet, he'd seen her use it when she melted the ice trapping him on the frozen continent, and again when she'd blown

her advisor into the wall of ice she created in the shelter.

"Don't be a douchepotato, you, you... douchepotato," she yelled.

The black dragon circled over, keeping his position of power in the air. He quirked his head to the side and then laughed. *That is an interesting mate you have, purple dragon. Take her to the ground and shift into your human form so we can talk. I swear the two of you will not be harmed.*

The decision to surrender was never an easy one, but if it would keep his mate safe, he had to. But the choice was not his alone. *My gem, the Black Dragon Wyvern wants us to land, and me to shift into my human form. We are trapped and surrounded, but I am prepared to fight for our freedom. What do you think?*

He could practically feel her savvy mind whirring, contemplating their situation. He loved her pure brain power. If they survived this night, he would pleasure her mind as much as her body when he finally got to claim her.

I'm tired of being bullied, but I don't like to fight, Genny said just to him. She scooted around in his claws so her head stuck out between his talons and shouted into the night sky, "How do we know we can trust you?"

"Because I am a Wyvern, first son of the First Dragon, and the Black Dragon Brotherhood is sworn to keep the world safe from all evils."

Genny jerked back, pushing herself against his leg. *"Whoa. He can talk in my head too? I don't like that. It feels weird."*

"Only true alpha Wyverns can speak to any other dragon like that. You have dragon heritage if you can hear him. Do you trust him?" Daughters of Dragons were rare but often became powerful witches. If her father or even grandfather was a Blue Dragon Warrior, Porfirio should know who he was. But no one in his Wyr had mated with a human and had a daughter in generations.

She didn't even seem to understand how to use her powers and denied that heritage. Perhaps her own parents were so afraid of those who hunted supernaturals that they hid her true powers from his father, the Blue Dragon Wyvern, and even from Genny herself.

Genny shot another icicle in the Black Dragon Wyvern's direction, although, with less force. A warning shot of her own. Such fierceness was so fucking sexy.

"Not good enough, douchepotato. What if you just up and decide we're evil? No go. What else you got?"

"You are not in a position to negotiate, little mate."

"And yet, I am." Her voice rang out with the self-assurance of a Goddess.

They may be in extreme danger at the moment, but Porfirio was so fucking turned on by her that when he did eventually shift back to his human form, he was going to be hard as a rock. For days.

"In the interest of getting back to my night with my own luscious mate, I will also offer that the Brotherhood is in alliance with the Troika pack, and we are trusted by the Wolf Tzar. If you won't take my word, perhaps theirs holds more power for you, since you are from here."

Genny's grip on his legs went much tighter. *"Uhh, how does he know I'm from Rogue?"*

"Your scent. I too could tell this was your home. Do you know these Troikas?" The Wolf Tzar was a powerful ally indeed. The more he learned about his mate, the more impressed with her he was.

"The Troika boys are all older than me, but they do own half the town and they've been known to be mistaken for the Russian mafia, if that's why he's calling one of them the Wolf Tzar. It's weird though. But what about this day isn't weird? Their mom owns a bookstore and coffeeshop across from campus that I go to a lot. She's a good person. If she vouches for this guy, then I guess we can trust them, at least for now."

The Black Dragon landed in the tree, a branch over

from the two of them. *"Your thoughts are very loud, little mate. But yes, Selena Troika will vouch for me. Although, I'm not sure how this turned into me having to prove I am the trustworthy one. You and your mate are the unknown entities here."*

Porfirio pulled on the only part of his element he had control over and made it snow directly over the Black Dragon's head. He shook it off, nonplussed, but also not viewing the flurry as a threat.

"I do believe my mate is going to enjoy getting to know the two of you. But I warn you now, if you hurt her, I will not hesitate to kill you."

Porfirio opened his mind to retaliate for that threat, but Genny interrupted him by shooting the Black Dragon in the forehead with a small icicle that exploded into slush when it hit him. "Right back at you, douchepotato."

"Hmm. Yvaine is going to love you." The Black Dragon Wyvern alighted from the tree and gave a jerk of his head for them to follow. The other dragons above continued to circle in a tight pattern that they would not be able to escape. *"I have informed the other Dragon Warriors here of your presence and all will be waiting for you at the base of the Dragon Tree. Be prepared to answer some questions, purple dragon."*

Purple. Ass. Dragon.

They could ask all the questions they wanted, he may not have the answers. Something very strange had happened to his world, and the worry that he was about to find out what sat on his chest like a mountain of ice.

"Now you're the one who is thinking loud." Genny stroked the fine scales of his underbelly, imbuing her positive energy into him with only her touch. *"Just so you know, I don't care what color you are, or whether you have answers to their questions or not. Their questions can eat a bag of dicks, and I'll tell them so if you want me to. You're not the only one who wants to keep their mate safe."*

"You're claiming me as your mate even though we haven't gone through the ritual, and I haven't given you my soul?"

"Yep. I don't know what any of that means, but I do know that from the moment I saw you through the ice, you and I were connected by something I didn't understand. I still don't. I never thought I could feel anything even close to what I do for you. Especially after, what, a few hours?" She snuggled against him, and if they weren't in the top of a tree, he would shift and hold her in his arms. *"But I do, and I don't care if it's unexplainable."*

Porfirio opened his claw and snuffled his mate's hair and the place where her coat covered the mark of his dragon on her skin. Would that be purple too? *"Fate brought us together for a reason. But even if we weren't fated mates, I would fall in love with you anyway."*

"Same, dragon of mine. Same." She held his snout in her hands and pressed a kiss to his nose. *"Now let's go meet some more dragons and tell them to piss off or I'll shoot their eyes out with my icicle finger guns."*

They took their time getting down to the ground, circling the tree in long arcs, slowly descending. On the ground, a whole host of supernaturals awaited them. Two Red Dragon Warriors, a Green, a Gold, a whole group of Black Dragons, and a wolf. Some had their mates by their sides.

The mates were human witches, save the one standing next to the Black Dragon. Porfirio could not identify what kind of being she was, but she had the scent of the Tuatha Dé Danann about her.

He set Genny gently on the ground, then shifted himself back into his human form. Everyone stared uncomfortably at the two of them, until the pretty blonde Tuath Dé woman rushed over and wrapped Genny into a giant hug.

"You brought us a fricking purple-butt dragon. I've always wanted a purple dragon, but no-oo." She drew the word no out like it was a song of its own. "Everyone said, 'There's no such thing as purple dragon, Yvaine. Don't be silly, Yvaine.' But I said, 'Look, if there can be dragons, and mermaids, and uni-freak-ing-corns, then there can be purple dragons.' And look, I was right. Told you so, Jett."

On the name Jett, the excitable woman raised just one arm and held her middle finger aloft at the Black Dragon Wyvern, who rolled his eyes.

Genny glanced over at Porfirio, still squished in the other woman's one-armed hug. *"Umm. Is this how dragon mates make friends? Because, awkward."*

DRAGONS, AND WITCHES, AND UNICORNS, OH MY!

Genny took another swig of her chocolate martini and waved at the cute bartender to bring her another. She was going to need more chocolate, and more fortitude, to continue this conversation. "Okay. So, let's see if I have this straight."

She looked around at the group of women sitting with her in the fancy speak-easy called The Sleepy Folk that she'd never had the guts to try to get into. The pies they served upstairs at the front though, were a staple in her diet.

Each of the women were so pretty and glamorous that Genny felt a bit like a potato sack sitting with them. But they'd all been so nice that she felt more welcomed than she ever had in... well, ever.

She pointed to the group of men with Porfirio,

standing at the bar. "That guy is the really big red dragon and the defacto king of the dragons. And he's your mate, right, Fallyn? And the guy standing next to him is the other red dragon and he's your mate, Jules, and second in command of the red dragons."

The woman who was mostly dressed in red leather, had a whole belt of daggers, and wore Christmas ornament earrings gave her a nod. "Yep. That's my Match."

Jules gave her a smile and sunshine sparkled around her like a freaking halo. "You got it. And I'm a Gold Witch with power over sun and wind."

Right. Witches. All the mates had magic powers like she did. Only they knew how to use them.

"And that guy is the green dragon and is second in command to the king of the green dragons, who are based in the Czech Republic, but you two live here, Fleur?"

Fleur was also from Rogue, and while they didn't exactly know each other, at least Genny recognized her. "Yep, that's Steele. He's called his Wyvern, Jakob, and they're on their way. You'll love Ciara. She's a white witch and can control all four elements."

Fleur waved at her mate and a daisy popped up out of her hair, because she was part nymph and that made her a Green Earth Witch who could do things with plants.

"Do me, do me." Yvaine, the woman who'd hugged the shit out of her when they landed, raised her hand, and bounced up and down in her chair.

"The big black dragon is your mate and he's half dragon, half demon, and has power over shadows?"

"It's just shadow," Fallyn interrupted and swirled a ball of darkness in her hand. "It's the element of the dark, where dreams live, as does the underworld."

Yvaine leaned over and stage whispered, "It isn't one of the four elements, it's special. Isn't that flipping H-A-W-T."

Or scary as hell. But somehow Yvaine's pure innocence made it all feel okay. No one would say what kind of being Yvaine was either, except that she wasn't an elemental witch.

"And your mate is the other bartender? The one that kind of looks like Jason Momoa?"

The beautiful woman in a white flowing dressed nodded and took a sip of her drink. Genny couldn't quite bring her name to mind. How embarrassing.

She glossed over that faux pas by continuing through her list of new things she'd learned tonight. "Those guys don't have mates or even names yet, because they've been living in Hell and have formed a gang or something to search for their missing souls?"

"Umm, almost," Yvaine said. "The Black Dragon

Brotherhood is partly to protect humankind from future threats from demons or whatever, but also to help each other not go crazy and darksideing-out while they search for mates to restore their souls. They are also excellent at planning parties."

Ohh-kay. They looked more like a motorcycle gang than party planners, but Genny had just about learned her lesson not to judge who or what anyone was by what they looked like.

"And you all have been living in Rogue, alongside werewolves, mostly the Troikas, who own half the town, and you have been since the battle to defeat the Queen of Hell." She sounded absolutely ridiculous. "Right?"

"Yep. But you know, there's not like a test later or anything." Jules flashed her thousand-kilowatt smile at her. You don't have to memorize everyone. I was a little late to the girl gang and I'm still learning it all too."

"I'm good at school and studying. This will help me get it all straight in my head. I'm better with books than people." If she wasn't going to be a scientist, maybe she could become a folklorist. "Someone really should write a How to Date a Dragon guide."

There was one thing she hadn't asked, because it was a bit too personal. She'd noticed that every single one of the women at the table with her were all not only gorgeous, but also plus size. Was that a thing with Dragons? They loved women with curves?

If so, she sure wished she known more dragons growing up. Being among other women who were soft and round like she was, but all had such glowing confidence and were proof positive that chubby girls got hot guys was... liberating.

"You go to BSU?" Jules, the Gold Witch asked.

"I do, or I did. I may have gotten myself kicked out and probably won't be able to graduate now. Good thing I have this witch thing to fall back on, huh?" She laughed even though none of that was funny. But if she didn't laugh, she'd cry.

The bartender came over with a tray of drinks and Genny snatched hers right out of his hand. The whole thing instantly turned into one solid ice cube. Crap. That was the third one tonight.

The woman in white touched her arm. "Your powers are tied to your emotions. Your dragon will help you with that. Just as you will help him with his new powers."

Genny glanced over at Porfirio. He and the other dragons were drinking beer that had green smoke at the top of the glass instead of a bubbly head. He looked as shell-shocked as she was. The guys were probably filling him in on everything that had happened over the past thousand years, and she didn't like that one bit.

She should be the one to help him acclimate to her world, and he could help her.

There was one more question she hadn't asked or gotten the answer to from the lovely women who'd instantly made her their friend. "I hope this isn't too forward to ask, but it's not like I can google it or go to the library to find out, so I'm just gonna ask and you let me know if it's too far."

The women all nodded and with open and accepting faces. "When you get intimate with your dragons, do they bite you and does your body go all supernova, or is that just me?"

The heat bubbled up across her chest, but also that that sensitive place Porfirio had bitten her. She reached up and touched the spot through her shirt and everything tingled when she did. All eyes were on her, but there was one set that she could literally feel staring at her.

A glance back to the bar, and she caught sight of that purple glowing amulet, and its same light reflected in Porfirio's eyes. His emotions, lust, need, and longing, filtered into her mind, just as if he was saying how much he wanted her.

Genny rubbed her fingers experimentally over the bite mark again, and whew, boy, she should not have done that in polite company. The heat that exploded between her thighs had her this close to moaning.

"If you keep that up, mate, I'm going to claim you right there on that table in front of all of our new friends."

She didn't wait for her new friends' answers. Hopefully she'd get to talk to them again later. Instead, she stood up so fast she knocked over both her chair and her frozen solid as a rock drink. "Ladies, I really enjoyed meeting you all, and I'm looking forward to this mate's club thing because I've never had many girlfriends, or really friends for that matter. But I think Porfirio and I have to go now."

Fallyn stood up with her and got right in the way. "I know what it's like to feel misplaced in time. Why don't you two come over for a meal this week with us? We're decorating the Christmas tree this weekend."

"Another one?" Yvaine giggled. "Fallyn, really, how many Christmas trees do you need?"

Fallyn looked at Yvaine and said with all seriousness, "All of them."

She really appreciated Fallyn's offer, but couldn't they all tell that if she didn't get with her man in the next twenty-seven seconds, she was going to die of lack of orgasms? That was a thing, right?

"Sounds great. I'll have my people call your people. Now, if you'll excuse me, I need to see a man about a dragon." Genny quickly crossed the bar, giving everyone a wide berth, because apparently most of them were werewolves, and went right up to Porfirio, placing herself between him and the rest of the men.

"Gentleman, uh, gentledragons, I'm afraid I have to steal my guy away from you. It's been a long day, night, whatever, and we have things to do that don't involve any of you. 'K, byeee." She took Porfirio's full beer glass out of his hand and set it on the bar. As she did, she caught the Jason Momoa bartender guy giving him a pointed look while tapping his chest.

Porfirio clasped his purple amulet and gave a quick nod. "I will remember your advice. Thank you."

No time to ask what that was about, and also, she didn't care. They were leaving, going home, and maybe not coming back out again for a week. Even better, not until after the holidays were over, and the new year was in full swing.

Not because she wanted to have loads of sexy times with Porfirio. Yeah, umm, not that. Anything but that.

She told the butterflies fluttering around her heart, lower belly, and between her legs to calm their tits. It had been a very trying day for both her and Porfirio, so he'd probably be tired and want to get some shut eye. If she was lucky, he'd be down for some spooning, and she should call that good.

Nope. No. She wasn't gonna think that way. That was grad-student-punching-bag kind of thinking, not a dragon's mate mindset. She's wanted Porfirio naked and all to herself from the word go and she was pretty damn sure, that's what he wanted to.

Genny didn't say another word because that would take up too much precious time. She grabbed Porfirio's arm and dragged him all of the three feet she was able to move him. He tugged her back, halting her mission, but made up for it by pulling her flush against his body.

His extremely hard body. Oh, yeah. He was definitely thinking exactly the same thing she was. Bed. Naked. Biting. Mating. Orgasms. Now.

She had to tip her head back to look up at him and found him staring down at her with dark lusty eyes. "Your protective instincts are so very appealing, my mate. It is sweet of you to come and save me from my brethren and their strange tales. But now I think it is my turn to take care of you again."

He brushed her messy hair behind her ear and rubbed one thumb down her cheek, continuing to trace her skin to the collar of her shirt.

Aww. Okay, she could calm her own tits for a

moment like this with him. "You're the one who just found out your whole world is something very different than what you thought it was. Let me be the one to be strong for you for just a little while."

"My world is not the only one that changed today. And you have no idea how much it means to me that you want to take care of me." His hand went down, down, down, tracing along her side, then sneaked behind and grabbed her butt. "But allow me to do the one thing that seems not to have changed in the last thousand years."

"What is that?" Oh no. Was it beer? Had she taken away his one solace? They had beer a thousand years ago, right?

"To claim my mate."

Hells to the yeah. If that meant what she thought it did, that was better than beer, and exactly the same thing she wanted.

"I accept. Let's definitely go do that. Right now."

Porfirio lifted her up into a princess hold and carried her through the remaining crowd while they cheered. He went directly up the stairs and out into the cool winter night. He paused outside in front of the pie shop, looked to the right, looked to the left, sniffed the air, and then headed in the direction of her apartment.

"A. Did you just smell where I live? And B. You can set me down now. I'm not exactly light as a feather."

Her looked at her like she was being ridiculous. "Your scent is unmistakable, even in this village of thousands of people. And no, it is my right and my pleasure to carry you across the threshold. Even if that wasn't my intention, I adore holding you in my arms just as much as I did my claws."

Fluttery flutter went those butterflies. She would never admit it out loud, but she got a kick out of him picking her up and carrying her around. He strode past the coffee place and through the alley, toward the small apartment complex behind the shops. He didn't even pause once, seeming to know exactly where to go.

"Much, much later you can show me your country's sights, so you may, what did Steele call it, ah, yes, so that you can blow my mind with the modernity of this place. But first, we shall spend the next week in your bed, where I can blow your mind."

"A week?" She about swallowed her tongue.

He nodded and studied the little porches and doors of her building, then went straight for number twelve. Which was of course, her house. "I would rather a month, but I think we would get hungry if I am not allowed to hunt for sheep or sea monsters as I did in my time."

"Yeah, even if Rogue is filled with all kinds of supernatural people, I've never seen any of them, so I'm guessing it would be bad if you flew out in broad daylight snatching up livestock for snacks. We'll just order DoorDash."

"I don't know what that means, but I'm sure you will teach me." Porfirio walked up to her door and lifted his leg as if he was going to kick it in.

"Wait, wait, wait. There's a key under that statue of a bearded dragon, uhh, the lizard. I'd rather we unlock the door, so I don't lose my deposit. Since I'm probably getting kicked out of school but will still have a billion dollars in school loans to pay off, I'm going to need every penny." She climbed down out of his arms, grabbed the key hidden under the ironic lizard, and unlocked her door.

"Do the people of your land still accept gold as payment?" She stepped into her little foyer, and he had to duck so as not to knock his head on her doorway.

She flipped on just the one light and led him around the corner to her bedroom. She wasn't waiting any longer than absolutely necessary to get naked with this man. "Kind of. But now it's made out of paper, or more often ones and zeroes floating through the digital universe."

He gawked at the apartment, her TV, the blinking

clock, and her mishmash of furniture. "If my gold can be converted to this paper, then I will pay for your schooling."

He was so incredibly thoughtful, and she did not exactly know how to deal with that. She certainly wasn't going to take advantage of him that way. But she was going to take full advantage of his amazing body and have him to the same to her. "I think you're going to need your gold. It's okay, I'll figure something out."

And she didn't want to talk about money anymore. To show him so, she pulled her first layer of warm clothing up and over her head, just like he had before. She tossed it on the bed before she decided she should do a little strip tease for fun.

Porfirio matched her moves and pulled his shirt off and tossed it over his shoulder. "I assure you, I have more than enough. Just my jewels alone would fill your home. I have carefully guarded my hoard and even if I have been gone for as long as you all say, I doubt anyone will have found it."

Screech. Stop. Hold up. "Just the jewels? Holy cannolis."

What was that she'd been thinking about an eccentric billionaire? Yet, she still didn't care about that even a hundredth as much as she did getting to touch and kiss and lick every inch of his body. "Umm, tell me all about your extravagant riches later, like, tomorrow morning after we have coffee."

He smiled down at her and her many layers. One sharp talon popped out of his finger, and he deftly sliced her shirts, undershirts, and bra open with a quick move. In a flash, she was naked from the waist up.

"And more sex. I will shower you with riches after I have claimed you so thoroughly you will have forgotten everything but how to scream my name as I make you come."

That sounded like the best plan ever.

PURPLE WORSHIP

*P*orfirio had never been a chaste man. Dragon Warriors were a horny lot, and he'd fucked his fair share of maidens, and mermaids alike. He knew how to tease and touch and taste to drive any woman to so many orgasms she forgot her own name.

And he couldn't remember any of those skills at the moment. Seeing his Genny fully naked, laid out for him with her hair across her pillow, her curves all begging for his hands, and he was the one who'd forgotten himself.

His cock and his dragon knew what they wanted though. So pure instinct was going to have to fill in the gaps, because his mind was a bowl of mush.

"You are absolutely the most gorgeous woman I

have ever seen in my life. How did I go so long without you?"

Genny blushed from her chest up, and he knew he would be paying her a lot more compliments just to see that pretty pink flush across her skin.

"I'm not great at accepting compliments, but for you, I'll try to be. Yours are the first that ever felt sincere to me anyway." She smiled at him in a way that was both shy and lusty.

"I would worship you, if you'd let me." Her body, her mind, and her soul were all of the divine.

"Oh, uh, yeah, I don't quite think that's necessary. I'll just take loving me if that's okay."

"I will do both at the same time. And I assure you, worshipping your body is entirely necessary. Let me show you." Porfirio pulled her legs toward him so her center was right at the end of the bed. Then he dropped to his knees before her and buried his face in her luscious cunt.

He licked her pussy lips, teasing her with his tongue, and was rewarded with whimpered moans and her fingers threading into his hair. "Please, Porfirio, don't tease."

"But I'm so good at it, my gem." He could spend hours, days, tasting and teasing her. The scent of her arousal was of that ripe persimmons he'd come to think of as uniquely her. "Let me make you come at least three or four times, then I will claim you."

Genny giggled and the tinkling sound went straight to his cock. Maybe just the three was enough, because he wasn't going to be able to wait much longer to be inside her. Her laughter transformed into urgent please once he sucked her clit into his mouth and lashed it with his tongue. Up and down, around and around, all while rhythmically sucking on her soft flesh.

Tiny flashes of purple light from his soul shard shot out into the room and sparkled around them like stars, or fireflies, or illuminated snowflakes.

"Porfirio, holy snowballs, that feels so good you're literally making me see stars." She pushed her hips against his mouth and released his hair in favor of fisting the blankets of her bed. "Don't stop, don't stop."

He was never stopping. His dragon pushed at him, rising up, wanting to take over, to bite, to mark, to claim his mate. But he'd promised her orgasms, and that's what she was going to get.

Genny's legs quivered, her pussy fluttered under his tongue, and if she didn't come soon, he would. Having her writhe in pleasure had his own arousal so near the breaking point that he'd be lucky not to come in his pants.

Wouldn't matter if he did, he'd be hard for her again in an instant. His delicious mate teetered on the edge of her orgasm, and he needed something to push her over. His mouth was currently very occupied, so he used their mental connection. "*Tell me what you need, my gem. I want to taste you coming on my tongue. I need you to come for me.*"

Without an answer, her back arched, and she screamed out his name as her body exploded into her orgasm. "Porfirio, yes, oh holy hell, yes."

"*That's my girl. Come for me. Spill your juices and let me taste your pleasure.*" His soul shard lit up the room in its purple light almost as brightly as the first time he'd touched her. It pulsed in time with the throb of her body, the beats of her clit against his tongue. He kept time with his tongue, flicking across her fluttering flesh, drawing her orgasm out until she collapsed back onto the bed.

Porfirio crawled up and over her, kissing and nipping across her thick thigh, the round curve of her belly, up to her soft round breasts, until he found his way to the purple bruise where he'd bitten her. If they hadn't been interrupted, he would have taken his time them to lick and heal her wound so that a proper mark of his dragon would have formed on her skin.

That was something he was happy to remedy now.

He gave the spot a scrape of his teeth, and Genny moaned.

"I guess all I needed was your voice in my head." She cupped his head and drew his face up to hers. Her eyes were dark with desire and yet bright with the light of her soul calling out to his.

He brushed his lips over hers, then took the kiss from light and teasing to urgent, pushing his way into her mouth, wanting her to taste herself on him. The noises she made let him know exactly how turned on she was by the way he shared the flavor of her orgasm with her.

"I think what you needed was not simply my voice, but to be told what to do."

She broke the kiss, and stared up at him with big, round, surprised eyes. "I absolutely hate it when the men in my life tell me what to do."

Uh-oh. He'd been sure that was what pushed her over.

"But with you, I... feel more like you're taking care of me than making a demand." She smiled and gave him a quick kiss that included a little nip to his own lips. "You're right. I did like that. A lot."

Genny squirmed under him, reminding them both that they had more fun to come. "I also liked when you called me your girl. I've never been anyone's girl before, and now I'm glad for that. I wouldn't want anyone else to call me that but you."

"You are my girl." He'd failed her already if she didn't know that." You're my mate, my everything."

"And you're mine too."

His dragon rose up so close to the surface, hearing her say the word mine.

Mark.

Claim.

Mate.

Give her your soul.

"I had plans to give you a whole lot more orgasms before I claimed you, but I can wait no longer." He stood quickly and undid the ties on his leggings, shucking them in one shove down his legs. His cock stood out, large, and hard, the head already beading with his seed.

"Where did you even fit that thing in your pants? You're huge." Genny stared at his cock with a bit of trepidation in her eyes.

He couldn't help but preen at her assessment. He wrapped his fist around the head and stroked up and down a few times, just to watch her eyes go wide. "All Dragon Warriors are well endowed. But don't worry, you'll be able to take me, and I promise you'll feel only pleasure.

"Gah. I wasn't worried about you fitting until you said that." She squeaked, but it was only a tease. "Good thing I've been wet for you for, oh, the last however many hours I've known you."

"And I'll make you even wetter as I make you come on my cock over and over." Starting right now.

Porfirio lifted his mate up by her waist and flipped her over so her pretty, plump, round ass was sticking straight up in the air. She looked over her shoulder at him and wiggled her backside deliciously.

He growled out her name. "Magenta. You are mine."

His control was gone, and his beast had taken over. "This first time, I must take you as my dragon needs, so the beast is satisfied you are marked, claimed, and mated. You must give yourself to me, let me make you mine." He grabbed her hips and used one knee to spread her legs wide. She may be wet, but he needed her soaking, dripping, so he could sink his cock all the way into her tight cunt.

He needed to fuck her hard and come so deep inside of her that she would be marked from the inside out.

Every dragon, demon, wolf, monster, or man would know that she belonged to him, and he to her.

Her pussy called to him, and he decided to use his cock to tease her until she was ready to come again. He gripped his member and notched the tip of it at her entrance, dipping into her wetness. He used his cock like a large finger and drew the juices out, then slid down through her folds to graze across her clit.

Genny dropped her head and groaned. "Ooh, oh, do that again and again, please."

"As you command, my lady." Someday when he had more patience and control, he'd let her grind herself on the length of his cock until she came. But not tonight. This was only the foreplay.

"Ugh, why is it so stinking hot when you say that? I thought you were the one who was going to tell me what to do."

"I will. When you need to be told." He was watching his cock slide through her wet flesh, so he got a perfect view of both her cunt and her tight little asshole clenching when he said that.

Relinquishing her control was a turn-on for her, but he would use that tool wisely. A few more thrusts, and he was covered in her juices and her thighs were slippery. His dragon could wait no longer.

"Are you ready for me, mate? Ready to be claimed?"

"Hells to the yeah, I am. I'm past ready. Take me, Porfirio. Make me yours." Her words had his soul shard glowing again, surrounding them in its purple glow. Their skin was caressed with the light and magic within, and he could hardly wait to give his soul over to her keeping.

He notched his cock at her entrance once again and this time he didn't hesitate. He pushed into her tight heat, inch by inch until he was seated as deep as he could go. The sensation of joining their bodies was so beyond gratifying and pleasurable that it took a minute before he found his voice.

"Fucking hell, you feel so good, my sweet gem. Look how well you take my cock." He withdrew only part of the way and drove back in. One of his hands crept over her ass and caressed the soft dimples in the small of her back. He pressed her further into the bed, needing to angle her exactly right so he could sink even deeper into her body.

"No more teasing me, Porfirio. I need you to fuck me."

"Ooh, my dirty mouthed girl. Be careful what you wish for because I'm going to give you everything you want." He gave her ass a hard slap, and quickly found a hard and fast rhythm.

"Yes, yes. Oh God, just like that. Fuck me harder, I need more of you. More." With each thrust, she pushed back against him so their flesh slapped together.

"Good girl, take my cock, take all of it." He was losing all control, fucking her fast and hard.

"So big, so full. I want more, I want all of you." Her words were long and drawn out, more of a pleasurable keen, than a coherent sentence.

He was so damn close to forgetting himself and letting his instincts fully take over. The dragon part of him wanted only to spill his seed and ensure his mark was on her skin. The man had to make sure that his mate found pleasure in their joining too. It was her gratification that mattered to him, not his own, not his dragon's. Only hers.

He'd fulfilled the beast's need to mount her and make her submit, now he'd make her come as was his true duty in the claiming. But he had to do it soon, or he'd be too lost to the sensations of her body claiming his.

Porfirio leaned over her and kissed the back of her neck. He alternated kisses and bites until he reached that special place at the crook of her neck where his true mark would be. With one foot up on the bed for leverage, he grabbed her by the shoulders and lifted her so her back was upright and pressed to his front.

The one downfall of fucking her from behind was that he didn't get to enjoy her tantalizing tits. He would be sucking on her nipples as he fingered her cunt later. For now, he had to be satisfied with a caress of them both.

"Put your hand between your legs and rub your clit while I fuck you from behind, mate." Any other time, he'd keep that delight for himself, but just this once, he was going to need both of his hands. One to hold her hip so he could continue to thrust into her at this brutal pace, and the other to hold her throat as he bit her, marking her once again. This time for keeps.

She did as he commanded, and soon she was breathing hard as her fingers found her core and intensified her pure need to come.

"That's my girl." She was his after all. Now and forever. "Don't stop until you come."

She panted and shook her head. "I want you to come with me."

If this taste of her was anything like the last, they would both be in nirvana soon. "Nothing can stop me from joining you in your climax this time, love."

He wrapped his hand around her throat and tipped her head to one side, exposing the spot where he'd bitten her. The magic he'd already imbued into her swirled on her skin but didn't form a mark. Before, he hadn't given her his all, his whole being, and this time he would.

Nothing would break them apart ever again.

SEX, LIES, AND THE TEN O'CLOCK NEWS

*W*hatever Genny had done in the dark under the covers with boys before this certainly was not sex. Not compared to what she and Porfirio we're doing right now. This was simply the most erotic experience of her entire life. But it was also the most meaningful, the most she'd ever felt connected to another person. The most everything.

He scraped his teeth across that ultra-sensitive area between her neck and her shoulder, and what she could only think of as pre-orgasmic tremors shook her body. If they were any indication, when she came, she was going to break into a million pieces, and only he would be able to put her back together again.

The purple snowflake-stars that had swirled around them before, reignited and turned her room into a blizzard of magic. Scales that matched the color appeared on the parts of Porfirio's arms that she could see, and suddenly a dragon's tail whipped around the side of her bed.

It snaked its way in front of them, and pushed her hand out from between her legs, replacing her fingers, with its cool tip. Porfirio ground words out in a husky growl. "I can't stand not giving you this pleasure myself."

The tip of his tail moved in time with the thrusts of his cock, and this was as close to being fucked by two men as she'd ever get. She very naughtily wondered what else he could do with his tail.

"Your erotic thoughts are very loud, sweet mate. I will make each and every one of those fantasies happen for you. Even the ones you think are too dirty to say out loud."

If getting a lover like him was her repayment for years of harassment and asshats up until now, honestly, she'd sign up for a second tour of duty. Because his dick was worth it.

His love was more than worth it. He was worth more than she could ever account for, until the end of time.

"I love you, Porfirio." She was so close to coming, she couldn't control her words, and switched to their mind connection. *"Not just for the way you utterly master my body, but for the way you love me right back."*

"I do love you, sweet gem, my mate. I thank the fates and the First Dragon for bringing me across time to find you." Another flash of purple light burst out, shadowed by Genny's own body. The amulet Porfirio wore burned hot against her back, but not uncomfortably. It heated her skin, just as his skin did.

He lowered his mouth to the nape of her neck again, and she leaned her head back against his other shoulder, opening herself for him. He controlled and consumed her body so completely, that she could do nothing else but give her whole being over to him.

His hand tightened around her throat, and she raised her hands to grasp his arm, not to tear him away, but to encourage this tight hold he had on her. She was in his care and felt entirely safe and cared for.

More magic swirled around them, and she felt his mouth change, the teeth he pressed against her skin shifted, from dull squared to the sharp fangs of her dragon. He sunk his fangs into her flesh and poured forth an energy so vibrant and erotic, she couldn't hold back any longer.

Her entire body exploded into the most epic of orgasms, shaking her to her core and back.

"I claim you, Magenta, as my love, my mate, the one true love that the fates have chosen for me. You are mine and I am yours for all of time, forevermore."

Porfirio's beautiful words filtered through her mind while he outwardly groaned, pouring his release into her, coming, and coming, and coming along with her. Their bodies were just as in sync as their minds, and now, their souls.

She didn't know how she knew that, but it was absolutely true. Their souls were one and nothing would ever be able to tear them apart.

Porfirio's tale slipped from between her legs and disappeared from her sight. He sighed with such a satisfied sound, it reached all the way from his chest to hers. He withdrew from her body, and turned her, picking her up in his arms again.

"Where do you think you're taking me now? Can't we just snuggle?" She whined and nuzzled into his chest anyway.

"You'll enjoy this one last thing and then we'll rest." He carried her the five feet from her bed to the tiny bathroom and held her up in front of the mirror.

"Hold on, I can't see a thing." She reached over to the wall and flicked on the light. The sconce above the sink illuminated and Porfirio jumped about a foot.

"Good Goddess, you are magical."

"Remind me to teach you about electricity tomor--" Her words trailed off as she caught sight of herself in the mirror. She had great sex hair, a very well-satisfied look on her face, and something entirely new on her skin.

From her throat, across her clavicle, and swirling down and around both her arm and her breast, was the most brilliant purple dragon tattoo. "Oh Porfirio, it's gorgeous, absolutely amazing. But how, when, how..."

It wasn't like she wouldn't remember getting a tattoo in the last couple of hours. Besides, except for naked times with him, she'd been clothed in so many layers a tattoo gun wouldn't have been able to get anywhere near her skin.

"This is the mark of my dragon on your skin. It shows the world that we are mated, it protects you, and extends my dragon's longevity to you. As long as I live, now so will you."

"What? You're not immortal or anything are you? Because you don't look a day over thirty."

"No," he chuckled. "I am just into my Prime, so with luck, I should live another three to four hundred years or so."

"Holy Roman Empire. That's unexpected. Someone really should write a book about mating with the supernatural."

He raised his eyebrows. "You're the most educated woman I've ever met. Maybe you should."

She raised her eyebrows right back at him. "I mean... it's not like I get to finish my degree or anything."

While snuggling did sound good, so did a shower, and she realized he would probably flip out when she showed him running water, especially hot and steamy. "It's my turn to show you something. Set me down and be prepared to have your mind blown."

"Ah yes, Steele's prophecy comes to fruition. Proceed to blow my mind." He waved his hand around in our magical fashion.

Genny leaned over the bathtub and turned on first the cold water and then the hot. She let the stream warm up and fill the little bathroom.

Porfirio did not look impressed. "You forget, little witch, that until a few hours ago, I too had control over the element of water. If you could not make hot water fill your fancy tub, I would be surprised."

"Well, you're no fun. I didn't know magic even existed until today, much less that I could do anything with water." She frowned at the filling tub and ice crystals formed all around the edges.

He cupped her cheeks and gave her a soft kiss. "Formerly being a Blue Dragon Warrior, I do still find the prospect of you in the element very arousing. Warm the water back up and let me bathe you, bring you to another orgasm or two, and then we will crawl into your soft bed, and I will hold you in my arms until morning light, or my morning wood, awakens us."

"Let's make it a shower so we can get to the snuggling faster." She concentrated on the shower head for a full minute, but not even a dribble came out. So, she flipped the knob to switch from the faucet instead of trying to use some weird magic she didn't really have any control over except in dire situations.

"Ooh, I like your rain of water." Porfirio climbed in and let the water wash over his chest and arms. The showerhead wasn't high enough to get his hair, but it was detachable, so she would help him wash it if he wanted.

Genny got in with him and it wasn't long before he found the bottles of body wash, shampoo, and conditioner. She pointed to the one they could wash with and held out a colorful mesh pouf that he just stared at.

It didn't take much longer until they were both slick and soapy and entirely too turned on again. "I'd love nothing more than to fuck you against the wall while the water rains down on us, but your soap and fancy floor are a bit too slippery to be safe. Let us rinse off and return to your bed."

It wasn't a minute after they got out before Genny's phone started ringing.

"What kind of animal do you have in this house that makes such a racket? Shall I kill it? I can smash the little beastie with my tail." Porfirio started throwing the clothes they shed around looking for the source of the noise.

"No, wait, no. That's my phone." Shoot. He wouldn't know what that meant. "It's a thing I use to talk to other people. Don't hit it with your tail."

She'd thought she'd left the thing in Antarctica when they escaped, but it must have been in the pocket of one of her many layered jackets. She rooted through the clothes Porfirio had sliced and diced and finally found the source of the sound. "Hello?"

"Oh, Genny, sorry. I was hoping I would catch you before I interrupted anything." Jules hurried to continue before Genny could even respond. "But I thought you'd want to know that Professor McFayden has been reported dead."

Oh, shitty shit shitsters. Had he died of his injuries when they'd busted him trying to interrupt their sexy times?

"How did you hear?" Genny paced back and forth while Porfirio glared at the phone.

"It's on the ten o'clock news. Turn on your TV."

Ten o'clock. It had been at least that late when the two of them had left the Sleepy Folk for her apartment and they'd been locked up in her apartment for hours since then. Did she maybe mean the morning news? Was it even light out yet?

Genny flicked on the tiny old TV set she kept in her room to watch reruns of Friends as she fell asleep. It only got local stations with the rabbit-eared antenna, but it did the job. The evening news popped right up, and the anchor appeared with a picture of McFayden above his left shoulder.

Porfirio growled and smacked the side of the TV sending it crashing to the floor. "That thing is dark shadow magic if I ever saw it. How was that small man trapped in there? We should call upon the Black Dragon Brotherhood to come here and try to free him."

"That is called a television. You wouldn't be the first to think it's some kind of magic, but I assure you it's science. Well, except for the actual programs. Those are questionable." She jogged into the living room and pointed to the slightly larger flat screen. "This is also a

TV, but it isn't mine, so please don't murder it. I promise we aren't in any danger watching the news."

Porfirio glared at the TV she pointed to but folded his arms. He was so very adorable in his protectiveness of her. She grabbed the remote and sat on the couch, patting the cushion next to her. The news was again on, but a different station.

"The surviving scientists say that McFayden appeared to have gone mad, raving about demons and dragons before he threw himself into the ravine. His body is yet to be recovered. Next up, we'll talk with the coach of our favorite local team, the BSU Dire Wolves, about their upcoming bowl game. And you know who is coming to town at the end of the week. Will we have a white Christmas? Join us after the break."

She clicked off the set and stared at the blank screen.

"Genny, your thoughts are very loud, but they are jumbled, and your scent has gone bitter like a rotten potato. Tell me what you're thinking so you may sort out your mind." Porfirio grabbed the blanket draped across the couch and wrapped her naked, slightly damp body in it.

Jumbled, rotten thoughts was an understatement. But he was right, talking them out would help. "Okay, two things. One, why would he throw himself into a ravine? The guy was a narcissist, but if he killed himself, he wouldn't be around to see the attention he was getting."

"I believe your advisor may have been possessed by demons." His voice was deadpan serious. "I was on the ice continent fighting the demon wyrms that were escaping from Hell via the ice capped volcano. You saw the remains of their bodies all around me when you melted the ice I was trapped in."

Right. Demons. Hell. Things that had nothing to do with science. But when she didn't understand some-thing, she knew to ask questions, create a hypothesis, test it, and evaluate. She could do that until she did understand.

"The black mineral deposits? Those were demon remains?" Gross. "But McFayden was obsessed with them. Even though he'd collected several samples, he'd sent me out there to get more. That's what I was doing when I found you."

She knew nothing about demons, but Porfirio did and so she had to trust that he knew what he was talking about. That answered one question and lifted the weight off her shoulders that they'd had anything to do with his death.

"We'll go back to that later, after I can talk to the other candidates on the team with us. But here's the other thing that is bothering me." This one probably couldn't be explained by demons. At this point, she was however, open to the answer being magic. "How long ago do you think we left Antarctica, the ice continent?"

"I'd guess about ten to twelve hours." He looked up and his eyes flicked about the room as he thought. "It's hard to tell how long we were in the air current that blew us here. But we'd left when the sun was high, and when we arrived, the sun had set."

Later, she would have to get out a map, a globe, and a lamp, and explain time zones. But regardless, she had about the same sense of the passage of time.

"Right. That's what I thought too. But if I think back to when I went out to the ice where I found you, which is the last time I knew the precise time, and now, which is apparently ten o'clock at night, either it's been about three hours, or twenty-seven."

He shook his head and his nostrils flared. "Neither of those make sense."

"No. They don't. And on top of that, I saw the clock in the pie shop when we left. It was just a few minutes before ten. But there on the news, it was ten O-seven. What is going on? Is this a dragon thing?"

"Not unless Dragon Warriors have learned some kind of new magic in the past thousand years while I was frozen in the ice. But they certainly didn't teach it to me."

"I have a hypothesis, but it's mostly based on gut feelings and not hard facts. I need you to kiss me, and maybe we have to have sex again to test it though." Genny looked at the clock in the foyer that now read ten-ten. She wrote that down.

"I am prepared to be a man of science for you."

This was going to be the most fun she'd ever had testing a theory in her life.

SEE WHAT'S BECOME OF ME

Time was a funny business. Porfirio had been caught up in its mysteries far too often for it to not have a significant effect on his life. Frozen in ice for a millennium, only to awaken to an age where magic wasn't magic but technology, and everything moved far too fast, and yet time slowed.

Like right now. He was kissing his mate, just as she asked him too, and he would live in this moment for the rest of time if he could. But the kiss and the moment were over far too soon.

Genny broke the kiss and glanced over to the time keeper hanging on her wall, then back at him. Her face was bathed in the purple glow of his soul shard, and her eyes were alight with the same from within. He hadn't even given her this piece of his soul, and yet she already held it in her keeping.

"Did you see that?" She pointed toward her time keeper. "The minute hand clicked back a whole minute when it should have gone forward. Are you doing that?"

"All I'm doing is kissing you and hoping for more." He pushed the strands of her hair still clinging to her face from their dip into the rain shower behind her ear so as to expose a little more of that luscious mark on her skin. "In fact, if anything, I think you're the one working some kind of magic. Look how my mark upon your skin glows with its own light from within."

"Fascinating. Do all the mate's marks do that?" She traced her finger over some of the dragon's lines and it writhed on her skin as if it was alive and reaching for her caress. "Whoa, and do they all do that too?"

"The mark is responsive to touch and will act to protect you as it is an extension of me. But I have never seen one that glows like that." He'd also never seen a purple one, but that was an entirely different matter.

"Here, let's experiment again, but I want to be able to observe us when we kiss. Move just a little bit this way so I can watch us in the mirror." Genny positioned him just a bit to the side and indicated toward a decorative mirror hanging on the wall.

"You think our actions of love and affection are creating some kind of magic?"

"Yes, that's my current working theory, but we need more testing. Lots and lots more evidence and data."

"If a kiss created the magic manifesting in the purple light and the oddity with the time keeper, don't you think something more intense would increase the affect?" He turned his mate so that she faced the mirror with her back to him and then dropped the blanket he'd wrapped her in to expose her soft, supple skin.

"Watch yourself in that mirror, my gem." They both stared at the image of themselves reflected in the mirror as he caressed the dragon mark, then worked his way down to her heavy breast. When he circled the nipples Genny's eyes first went wide, but then drifted shut, reveling in his touch.

"Watch, Magenta. See what I see when I touch you."

Her eyes fluttered open again, but instead of watching herself, she caught his eyes and they fell into each other's gazes. His hands roamed all over her body, working their way down from her breasts to her soft belly that he hoped one day would hold their son or daughter, and then lower, to the apex of her thighs.

As he did so, the dragon on her skin glowed, the

shard at his neck matched the light, and their eyes filled with the same illumination. When he skimmed his fingers across the soft hair covering her cunt, and then dipped them inside her folds, finding her clit and circling it, the light intensified.

"If you keep doing that, I'm not going to be able to keep my eyes open." She arched her back and tilted her hips, pushing her ass against his already hard cock.

"I promise to watch for the both of us." He did want to see what the strange purple magic was going to do, but even more, he needed to watch his mate ride his fingers, take her pleasure from his touch, and come again just for him. Only for him.

Porfirio worked her clit, pinching, stroking, circling, and finding exactly the way she liked to be touched. While almost all of his attention was on Genny and her pleasure, he had promised he would observe the magic around them for her too.

With each passing moment, as her orgasm approached, the light that filtered into her home from the window to the outside joined with that of their purple glowing magic and changed. What should have taken hours for the night to pass into the light of day and then the sun to set again, came and went in only a few heartbeats. It didn't take long before her breaths became moans, and then cries, and then the beautiful soft whimpers as she came on his fingers.

She leaned back against him with her eyes shut and satisfaction written across her features. He pulled his fingers from her cunt and brought them up to her lips, painting them with her own release. "Open your eyes, sweet mate. Come back to me and see the magic we have created together."

She blinked a few times, and he pushed his fingers into her mouth just to watch the delicious way her eyes darkened at tasting herself on him. He too wanted a taste and turned her in his arms, taking her mouth in a deep kiss, dueling with her tongue to take back every bit of her juices.

He felt the magic flowing around them this time, no longer needing to see it in action. He understood now that whatever was happening around them came from the combining of their two souls, and that it was a new and unique power, one that no dragon or witch had ever seen before.

When Genny finally pulled her lips from his, she smiled, stretched, and looked at her time keeper. "Huh. It's the exact same time as when I last looked. Whatever we're doing, it seems to slow or freeze time, in that particular minute."

"I agree that the magic we are creating has something to do with time, but if you'll check again, we did not slow time, we sped it up. Days have passed. I watched the sun rise and set once and again."

"What? Whoa." She pulled from his arms and grabbed her tiny box that sang like an injured animal. She touched it, making small lights appear and images flash across it. "Yikes. It's already the weekend before Christmas. How the heck did that happen? Don't answer that."

She held up a finger and her eyes flicked back and forth, back and forth, her mind working through the information. After a few more moments, she tipped her head to the side, gave it a small shake, and said, "Time travel? Could it possibly be? Dammit. I knew I should have studied physics."

He didn't know what physics was, but it sounded like physical, and he was always down to study her body. "Yes, I agree. We should do some more of your experiments to find out."

She giggled as he swooped her up into his arms to take her back to the bedroom, but she squirmed to get out of his hold. "While I hope to spend a lot of time... ha, time, anyway. I hope we can do lots and lots more experimenting, but I'd like to get some other sources of information. That woman, Fallyn, said that she had experience with being out of time. Do you think she might know something?"

If he had been left on his own to figure out this magical mystery, he would never have gotten nearly as far as his mate had already. So smart. "According to her mate, the Red Dragon Wyvern, she is a very powerful Red Witch who comes from the line of witches who have the power to draw out a portion of our souls to fuse with the First Dragon's and create our soul shards. She probably knows more than we can imagine."

"They did invite us over for dinner. Let's go talk to them." She tapped on her communication box again, and a moment later it made a tinkling sound like a tiny bell. "Okay. We're all set. They're expecting us in an hour."

"I know something we can do for the next hour." Several somethings.

Genny backed away, laughing. "No. No, no. Don't touch me, don't kiss me, don't say anything even the slightest bit naughty, don't even wink at me. We don't understand yet how this works and I don't want to get all turned on and find out we jumped forward an entire year or..."

Her eyes went wide and her thinking face came back. "Or a thousand years. You weren't, umm, you know like, doing anything arousing when you got frozen in the ice, were you?"

He grabbed his cock and gave it a few strokes. "You mean, like this?"

She took a few steps back, but her eyes were fixed on his hand. "Yes. But also no, don't do that. I don't want you to time travel without me."

He laughed and let his member go. "I was not touching myself or engaging in any other sexually arousing activities back then. I was fighting a horde of demon wyrms. The last thing I remember was destroying the final wyrm and then, the next thing I knew, I saw you. But it makes sense that I slipped forward in time and wasn't frozen in the ice for a thousand years."

"Yeah, that makes way more sense." She quirked her head to the side, considering it all again. "I wondered how you didn't die frozen like that in the first place. But if it was only for a moment and then I thawed you out, well, I'm guessing dragons have enhanced healing and protective systems innately, since you do things like breath fire and ice and crazy stuff that would kill most humans."

They dressed again, her in considerably less layers this time. When she went to put on her small pants that she wore under her garments, he snatched them away and tossed them over his shoulder. "You don't need those. They'll just be in my way later."

Genny found him a shirt made of a lightweight, finely woven fabric called a t-shirt, and the softest leggings he'd ever touched in his life, called sweatpants. Both were from her wardrobe in a section she called her pajama drawer. They were a bit snug on him, but infinitely more comfortable than his own clothes.

He liked the way the leggings showed off the outline of his cock for all to see.

"Oh my. Yeah." Genny gawked at his lower half in a way that had him preening for her. "I'm buying you a load of gray sweatpants to wear, even if the whole town will stare at you scandalously."

She put on a puffy purple coat, and it was ridiculously hard for him to keep his hands off her. In the past, blue had been the color he was most attracted to but seeing her in a garment that matched that of his shard and her dragon mark sent his dragon into a frenzy of need.

"They don't live far, but it's chilly out, so I think we should drive. This is going to be another of those things that's probably going to blow your mind. Come on. Let's go see if you even fit in my car." Outside, behind the row of homes she lived in, was a small, round cart-like thing with wheels, but there was no animal to pull it.

"Why don't I just shift and fly us over to where they live?" He eyed the cart as she opened a part of it and got inside. He wasn't going to fit.

"Try to squeeze in here. We can't go flying everywhere, even if half the town is supernatural. Half isn't, and I don't want us to get caught." She waved him over and he acquiesced.

It took several tries, and a whole lot of effort, to fit himself into the cart. He'd tried head first but had ended up with his face in her chest, which he enjoyed, but she said wouldn't work because she couldn't steer. Then he tried feet first, but there was no place for his knees to go. Finally, she opened something called a sunroof, and he stepped in through a hole in the top of the cart and stood upright like the chariots of the Romans.

"Now bend your knees and put your butt on the seat. I'm not driving through town with you looking like we're going for a joyride."

He finally managed to slide down and sit next to her with his knees in his chest. "Now what?"

She shook her head, touched the panel in front of her and the cart rumbled and growled beneath them. "Is it alive?"

"Umm, sort of. I'll add combustion engines to our learning list for you later." She gripped a wheel directly in front of her and the cart moved forward. They moved through the streets of her village at a rate much faster than walking or running, but not as fast as he could fly.

When they finally arrived at the Red Wyvern's home, it took him almost as long to extricate himself from the cart as it did to get in. Genny stood next to the thing watching him, and only when he was by her side did, she point back at it. "Umm, wasn't my car silver when we left?"

He nodded but frowned. The cart was now a deep shade of purple. "It appears this interesting new element wishes to be pervasive in our lives."

Fallyn waved at them from the front door to her home, and they joined her inside. "Everyone is out back waiting for you two. Match likes to barbecue when we have people over. And when we don't. He just likes to play with his fire if I'm honest."

"Everyone?" Genny asked.

"Yeah. When you two showed up, disappeared again, and your house was nothing but a ball of purple light inside, we figured we'd better call an AllWyr. The five Wyverns and their mates are all here now." Fallyn led them through the house and into a garden behind her home.

A group of the Black Dragon Brotherhood were just leaving. Jett called after them. "And Neo, after you recover the bodies from Antarctica, I want you to head up the team to investigate what happened to that family here in the U. S, and report back to me. Something more is afoot that we know."

A giant brooding man saluted Jett and gave her and Porfirio a nod as he passed them. "Don't worry. We'll find out what happened and put a stop to it."

Antarctica? Bodies? Witches? What happened while he and Genny were making their bond?

All eyes turned to them, and Genny grabbed his hand. "I feel like I'm about to defend my dissertation to one tough crowd."

I WANT A PURPLE DRAGONPOTAMUS FOR CHRISTMAS

*P*orfirio squeezed her hand and spoke into her mind. *"That is the Blue Dragon Wyvern. He is the spitting image of my younger brother."*

His emotions came through just as loud and clear, but they were a jumble. He was surprised and anxious. She didn't think her dragon man knew how to be nervous.

Genny glanced over at the brown-skinned man who had that same look of a Pacific Islander as Porfirio did. He wore an outfit of bright blue and sported blue tattoos. Oh, he was probably Māori. That would make sense if Porfirio's people had been living in New Zealand at least a half millennium before it was colonized by the west. She whispered back. "Is that a bad thing?"

"No. It's just that, had I not slipped forward in time to you, I would have become Wyvern of the Blue Dragons." His hand released and tightened around hers, and she could quite literally feel the beat of his heart pounding in his chest. "It is a position that is passed down among first sons. But I suppose when I went missing, that is a role my younger brother had to assume. It's strange to think about all that must have happened in my absence."

"Do you want to go meet him, or do you want me to run interference, so you don't have to talk to him?" Nobody was going to make her, or her dragon do anything they didn't want to.

He stilled and leaned against her. "My fierce, sweet gem. Ready to defend me even against the most powerful dragons in the universe. I love you for it."

"I got you, boo."

"And I you. Now let's go meet what I'm guessing is my great, great, great nephew." They strode over to the group, and they all fell silent. "Wyverns. I am Porfirio Kahurangi, son of Kupe, formerly of the Blue Dragon Wyr."

Everyone's faces went from Porfirio to the man he'd identified as the Blue Dragon Wyvern.

"I am Kaiārahi Tarakona Puru, Blue Dragon Wyvern. My great grandfather quite a few times removed was Kupe. But he had no other sons besides my lineage. How can you be who you say you are, and in this place and time, when Kupe lived a thousand years ago?" The Blue Dragon Wyvern's questions were not accusing, but more curious. "By all reports, you aren't a Blue Dragon Warrior at all. Your scales and magic are purple."

"Yes, Wyvern. It appears I am now a purple dragon and am out of place in time and with no Wyr, even though my father was Kupe. I cannot tell you how any of this came to be, but my mate and I are trying to figure that out." Porfirio put his arm around her, and she gave the circle a wave.

"Oh, I don't know about not having a Wyr," another man who looked vaguely familiar said. Genny felt like she should recognize him, but the memory was just out of reach. She'd have thought she'd remember meeting someone who looked like Jason Momoa, but who had a prosthetic arm.

"Maybe you just need to go in search of the other Purple Dragon Warriors." A beautiful olive-skinned woman in long white flowing robes added. "Perhaps they too are lost in time."

The five Wyverns all looked at each other, and Genny guessed they were using some kind of mind speak amongst themselves. As a unit, they turned to her and Porfirio. That wasn't intimidating at all.

Match, the one she remembered was the defacto king of the Dragon Warriors, stepped forward and placed a hand on Porfirio's shoulder. "We can't have a Dragon Warrior without a Wyr, and since you're the only one of your kind, we name you the Purple Dragon Wyvern. Welcome to the AllWyr Council."

Porfirio blinked a few times and looked just as shocked as when she'd turned on the TV for the first time. "I am honored Wyverns. Thank you."

"I'm sure we all have lots of questions for our new friends. So, let's sit and eat and talk, and make plans for a new Wyvern Christmas wedding, hmm?" A pretty blonde woman with sparkling green eyes that matched both her dress and the jacket of the man she was standing with, waved everyone over to a table so elaborately decorated, that it looked like this back yard winter barbecue was professionally catered. "Come, sit next to me and Azy, we haven't gotten to meet you and welcome you to the mate's club yet."

"Uh-oh," the pale woman in blue standing with Ky-uh-something-or-other rolled her eyes and smiled. "You're about to be initiated by fire, I mean wedding planning."

A woman with long, black, tight curls, dressed all in gold shook her head, but also grinned. "Can't hardly be a Wyvern's mate if Ciara doesn't plan some kind of wedding shindig for you."

"Or an elaborate birthday and love party. Those are fun too," Yvaine, whom she'd met the other night, added.

"Shush, the lot of you. You all loved the weddings and birthday parties I planned for you. No reason we can't do a purple-themed one too."

"Somebody loved them," the woman in gold said.

Genny sat down with the women and Porfirio once again joined the men. He was much more relaxed this time than at the bar the other night, but she was going to keep her eye on him. She introduced herself and learned everyone's names.

"Magenta, I love it. Suits you perfectly. Although, I'm gonna stick with calling you Genny." Yvaine snacked on a pile of carrots she'd snagged from a vegetable tray. "Of course you'd become the mate of a freaking Purple Dragon Warrior. What's your last name?"

"Kronos."

The girls all went silent. "What? Oh. Ohh. You think that means something?"

The woman in white poured them all cups of

steaming hot tea. "There are never any coincidences when I go in search of a mate for my dragon sons."

Ciara, the Green Dragon's mate, picked up the conversation as if no one else had even said anything. "Fallyn, can we use your house and your four-hundred and twenty-seven thousand Christmas ornaments as decorations?"

Fallyn made a face that Genny was sure meant that Ciara should fuck off. "As long as you return them all and remember that they are all mine."

"Yes, yes," Azy, the Gold Dragon Wyvern's mate, waved her hand. "Every Christmas ornament in the whole world belongs to you or will by the time you're through with them."

Clearly these women were all great friends and a warmth spread in Genny's chest.

The woman in white, whose name Genny hadn't quite caught, leaned over, and whispered in her ear. "She doesn't collect just any ornament willy nilly. Most of them contain spells within them."

"Like magic spells? That's cool."

"Yes. Most of them. Not all. Like this one. It's for you." The woman handed an ornament to Genny. It was a clear bulb with a glowing purple ring swirling and spinning in the center.

Genny examined the ornament and admired its

beauty. "Oh, it's so pretty. Thank you." When she looked up again, no one was there. Who had she been talking to?

"The only thing I wonder about is the challenge of the mate's ring." Jada handed a plate of tiny powdered-sugar donuts around the table. "With Porfirio being newly dubbed a Wyvern and all, do you think the White Witch will hide a ring for Genny to prove she's his one true mate?"

Porfirio's eyes met Genny's and his face broke out into a huge grin. "I believe that's already happened."

"It has?" She didn't remember doing any challenge.

"Yes, sweet gem." He walked around the table and knelt beside her. "What are you holding in your hand?"

Genny lifted the Christmas ornament, but it wasn't an ornament any longer. She held only the glowing ring in her hand.

Almost everyone else's jaws dropped open in awe and amazement, except for Yvaine's. "That sneaky witch. You gotta love her."

Porfirio clasped Genny's hands in his and brushed a kiss across her lips. Purple light exploded all around them and in a blink, the world around them changed.

"Ooh. Look, everybody. They're back." Ciara patted Genny on the back. "That was perfect timing. But I'd expect nothing less from a Dragon Warrior and a Witch whose element is time."

"Oh, how long were we gone? We really have to figure out how to get some control over those jumps." Genny looked around and saw that all the same people were there, but they were all dressed in colorful formal wear.

The back yard still had the long table with its fancy decorations, but the flowers and napkins were all purple. There were also a dozen Christmas trees with twinkling lights and mostly purple decorations set along one side with rows of chairs facing them. There was a beautiful pergola front and center, with carvings of dragons all over it.

The whole place looked set up for a wedding.

"Porfirio, since you're down on one knee and holding a ring, why don't you give Genny that fun human experience and ask her to marry you?" Ciara said and then stepped away.

Porfirio looked up at her and wrinkled up his nose. "Dragons don't marry, we mate. That is much more binding."

One of the other Dragon Warriors shouted from the gathered crowd. "Do it anyway or you'll never hear the end of it. I promise."

"Do you want me to do this, sweet gem? I will absolutely ask you to marry me if it would please you."

Genny agreed with him that the mating bond they'd formed felt so much stronger than any sort of marriage certificate, but she did like the idea of getting to say vows in front of their new friends who already felt like family. She wished her parents were here.

"I would like to marry you. You and I both know we belong to each other, let's share that loveliness with everyone else."

"You're so smart." Even though he didn't know the etiquette or ritual of the modern-day proposal, he did everything exactly right anyway. Porfirio took the glowing ring from her and held it out like an offering. "Will you marry me, Magenta, mate of my heart and of my soul?"

"Yes."

He leaned forward to kiss her, but Ciara slipped her hand between the two of them before their lips could touch. "Wedding first. Kissing and time travel later."

Ciara whisked Genny away, and the guys took Porfirio. Like only the absolute best wedding planner could, it looked like Ciara had anticipated everything, including a last-minute bride and groom. She had a gorgeous lavender wedding dress waiting for Genny, and apparently a tux waiting for Porfirio.

When Genny got the whole regalia on, she smoothed her hands over the skirt and stared in the mirror. "How did you know my size? It fits perfectly and isn't even uncomfortable like I thought a wedding dress would be."

"That's my job, and my delight. Now, let's go get you married so we can get to the best part."

"The honeymoon?"

Ciara laughed. "I was thinking cake, but yeah, the honeymoon is probably going to be more fun for you than a white chocolate cake with purple elderberry filling, and only the purpliest of edible flowers for decorations."

That did sound pretty damn good.

Ciara handed over a bouquet of purple flowers and guided Genny back to the yard where her perfectly styled purple and Christmas themed wedding was ready and waiting.

"Thank you for doing this. I never dreamed I'd find the right one, much have a lavish wedding like this."

"It's all part of the service." Ciara gave her a dismissive wave. "Besides, it was definitely my pleasure. Okay, your dad is waiting to walk you down the aisle just over there. Good luck."

Genny's heart melted when she realized her parents were here. Her father stood in the doorway out to the backyard, dressed in a tux himself, with a deep blue tie and pocket square.

"Hi, daddy. Did you meet Porfirio? Are you and mom going crazy wondering what's going on? I promise I'll explain--"

"No need sweetheart. We know. We're the ones who've been keeping secrets from you." Her father took her hand, and his eyes went a brilliant blue, then his face slowly changed, sprouting scales, fangs, and a snout.

"Dad! You're a Blue Dragon Warrior?"

He shifted back and chuckled. "I am. We'll talk after about why your mother and I kept it a secret from you. But first, I think your mate is waiting, and I'd hate to disappoint the Purple Dragon Wyvern on your wedding day."

As her father walked her up the aisle, a gentle snow fell around them. But Genny wasn't cold. Not even a little. She had too much love and warmth in her heart.

When she got to the front of the aisle, Porfirio took her hand and kissed it. "I'll save more for later, but for now, I'd like to live in this moment with my beautiful bride."

They turned and faced Match, who held an ancient book in his hands. "Repeat after me."

They both nodded and Match began to speak in an ancient language, but somehow Genny had no problem understanding. ""*Ni*, Magenta Kronos, *cad men anna ni gud* Porfirio Kahurangi."

She said the words, meaning every bit of the vow that she now belonged to the Dragon Warrior.

Match turned to Porfirio and said the phrase for Porfirio to repeat.

Her amazing mate looked deep into her eyes and said the words claiming her for his own and vowing to protect her as was his duty, *"Ni*, Porfirio Kahurangi, *gud tammabuki, cad men anna ni ilati sinnis*, Magenta Kronos."

Another man standing behind Match cleared his throat and tapped his chest, giving Porfirio a pointed look.

"There's one more thing I have to give you, my mate, my sweet gem." He took off the amulet he wore around his neck and placed it over her head. "I give you my soul, for your safe-keeping. It is all that I am, and all that I have. Now it is yours, forever."

The purple shard of his soul threw out a brilliant light and lit up Genny's tattoo. Porfirio leaned forward and kissed her, not holding back this time, but pouring all the passion they shared into the kiss.

The world around them dissolved and disappeared, and Genny felt the passage of time go by. But as they broke the kiss and the light faded away, she thought of the moment they were missing and boop, they were back in their time and place, among their friends and family.

The man who'd prompted Porfirio to give her his soul shard grinned and shook his head. "I told you to give her your soul. Now you have control over your element. Have fun toodling around time. I can't wait to see how that goes."

He winked at them and poof, the man became a rainbow of sparkling snowflakes swirling around them both.

Genny giggled and tugged Porfirio back down for another kiss. This one lasted for all the rest of time.

NEED a little more time with Genny and Porfirio? Get this bonus epilogue when you join my Curvy Connection email newsletter.

Want to find out what mission Neo and the Black Dragon Brotherhood are on?

Grab Tamed, the first book in the spin off series and keep getting your dragon fix. Turn the page to read the first chapter now.

TAMED: CHAPTER ONE

CRASH INTO ME

Too many of Neo's muscles and ligaments were injured for his dragon to heal them. His wings couldn't keep him from losing altitude and he was falling behind the rest of the Black Dragon Brotherhood. The only things still intact in his entire being were his shard and his soul. And he wasn't entirely sure about his soul.

Fuck. He hadn't said anything to the other warriors of the brotherhood about how badly the new threat they'd discovered had destroyed his body. He was supposed to be their leader, and here he was, the first one to fall. He'd borne the biggest brunt of the recent attack, and his dragon hadn't been able to heal him.

Neo? Boss man. You okay? Apollo was already using

his power over the wind to keep Neo in the air. They were only halfway through the flight from the scene of the battle on the west coast, trying to fly back to Rogue. They had to let Jett and the other Wyverns know about the strange shadow warriors.

Dammit. He did not want to admit that he was hurt. Great fucking way to lead their first mission. First a failure to stop the earthquakes created by the shadow, then a retreat from warriors they couldn't even touch, and now he was going to crash like a youngling who didn't know how to fly properly.

Apollo, you're going to have to use your powers to get the others back to Rogue as fast as you can. Leave me. The Brotherhood and the Dragon Wyrs need to know we weren't able to fight off these shadow warriors.

What? Me? Apollo half fell out of the sky himself.

As the heir to the Gold Wyvern, the kid needed to dragon up. He had a lot of courage, but also a lot of fear about who and what he was. Join the club.

Yes. I'm not going to make it. You have to make sure the Dragon Warriors and the wolves are prepared to meet this shadowy threat from Hell. He'd done everything he could to smash their attackers to bits with his fists, and then tried using his tail and claws, but he had no idea how to hurt them. No one did. Every shifter or magical being they'd questioned was scared to death because nothing worked to defend against the shadow coming and stealing their souls.

They certainly weren't demon wyrms, or even Annunaki, because no known enemy created wounds with weapons made of shadow, wounds that wouldn't even heal when Neo shifted into his dragon form.

Neo assumed the forces of Hell were behind the attacks on the supernatural beings and his small crew. Unless Kur-Jara wasn't as reformed as Match had claimed and was still working with Ereshkigal.

Shit, the Black Dragon's name wasn't even Kur-Jara now. He wasn't even the Black Dragon anymore. Dude needed to choose a name. All of his crew besides Apollo were still nameless bastards with numbers for nicknames. He wasn't even a good enough leader to inspire them to pick what to be called.

The dragon inside him roared out as a new spike of pain shuddered through his wings. He dropped a thousand feet through the sky before Apollo's wind straightened him back out. Shadow be damned, he was going to crash trying to fly over these snow-peaked mountains.

If he died before finding out who or what these shadow warriors were, and why they were stealing souls, any Annunaki who even tried to judge him and take him to the afterlife would face the sharp end of his tail. He wasn't going down without a fight.

Except he was. Soon.

Pain jabbed at his chest and his dragon shuddered. This was it he was about two seconds from crashing into the side of the mountain. *Listen up, team. I'm going to attempt to land and hide in the forested area ahead until my dragon can heal these wounds. Continue to Rogue, New York, and report in with Jett. Getting him the info about the shadow creating those earthquakes is the key to hunting the soul stealers. I'll catch up as soon as I can.*

He got "yes, sir" from his three brethren, a "got it" from Apollo, and a grumble from Not-Kur-Jara. That hell spawn was going to be the death of Neo. He directed his dragon voice only to Not-Kur-Jara. *You make sure Apollo gets back safe. You got it?*

Yup. A one-word response was more than he usually gave, so Neo would take it. He didn't have time for cranky-ass bullshit.

His wings folded under a new wave of pain and he took a steep dive. Neo pushed his body to stretch his wings out again, praying for a response, but what he got was gusts of wind jerking him around, literally. *Apollo. Leave me. Use your wind to get to Rogue. Now.*

The other dragons yelled warnings, but Neo didn't have the time to care. He was too busy trying not to die. He narrowly missed the top of one peak and caught his talons on the snow and rock. That sent him careening into the valley below. *Aw, fuck me.*

Join the Black Dragon Brotherhood they said, it'll be life-changing they said.

He didn't need life-changing, he needed a damned lead on the shadow warrior threat and a way to defeat them. If one more family of wolves, coven of witches, or any other supernatural being came to the Black Dragon Brotherhood pleading for his help...No, he wouldn't think of those who grieved their sons and daughters, fathers and mothers now. If he lived through this day he'd vow to rescue as many as he could and avenge those he couldn't.

First, he had to survive, the dragon inside of him taunted.

The Rockies' enormous white-tipped peaks were too much for Neo to cross. Dark clouds engulfed his body and bounced and bumped him around until his teeth rattled. It was only a few seconds until he broke through the cloud cover and saw the land below growing in front of his face.

The miles of green trees and snow-capped mountains were so unlike the confining darkness of Hell. If fate decreed that he had to die anywhere, this would be where his soul would most be at rest, out in the open where he could see the sun and stars for evermore.

Not that he was giving up. No way. Never. If he could just level out to an angle that wasn't quite so steep, he might be able to skim across the land and stop, upright and alive. That is, if no large structures or natural formations blocked his path. Like the side of that mountain.

Shit.

Neo took a deep breath and drew his wings and body in for his last-ditch effort. A cannonball crash. He hadn't tried one since he'd learned to fly as baby demon dragon, and even then, he hadn't been good at it. Jumping butt first into a pit of crunchy lava stone from the ceiling of his cave and smashing his a forty-ton grown-ass dragon body into the side of the mountain were not the same thing.

He folded in his tail and tucked his wings around his body to make himself into a ball. He'd flip over at the last minute so his armored scales on his back would take the brunt of the crash landing. He figured he had less than ten seconds until he crashed.

Seven—

He cursed the shadow warriors one last time and pulled in his wings. Years of living Hell and battles alongside the Wyverns had given him more strength than most Dragon Warriors. He called upon the First Dragon to imbue him with more. He was going to need a lot of his supernatural healing powers to survive this crash. This was going to hurt like hell. Or worse.

Six—

His body continued its descent, but without his wings to guide him the turbulence pushed him into a downward spiral. His muscles strained. He needed to try and crash into some snow instead of the jagged rocks. He twisted just enough to adjust his trajectory toward the highest snowbank, but that put a flock of birds directly in his flight path.

He tried to roar at the little beasts to get out of the way, but the wind took his breath away. The first one struck his side and small explosion of his scales shook his tail. Shit.

He careened out of control and another bird hit his wing, taking out a chunk of flesh with it.

"Come on, come on." Maybe if he sweet talked the universe into helping him not die, she'd do his bidding. Not like he'd had much luck sweet talking the ladies.

Five seconds to impact—

Sweat beaded on his brow and snout, dripping between his scales. His own efforts weren't going to be enough to save him. Where were the First Dragon and the White Witch when you needed them? Maybe they'd come to his aid if he made them a deal. "I swear to give everything I've got to defeating this new shadow enemy. Gimme just a little back."

The ground rose up faster and faster. No way he was going to hit the snow patch now. Four seconds—

A gust of wind pushed at his belly, and he leveled out by the tiniest degree. Maybe the universe or the First Dragon were listening. This could be a good or a bad thing. Neo's muscles trembled and shook under the absolute exertion of trying to get his wings to stretch out and guide him along the small eddy of wind. "That's it. Thank you, whoever you are."

Three seconds—

He skimmed the tops of a clump of dark evergreen trees, then dipped into them. The sound of breaking branches and the trunks smashing on his face, sides, and tail were louder than the roars of his fellow dragons and hurt more than the demon wyrm's fire in battle.

Two—

The last thought that flashed through his mind before impact wasn't of his brethren, their battles, or his life playing before his eyes. It was that the shard hanging over his heart glowed with the light of a whole damn volcano's worth of fire.

The light flashed as bright as a single flame in the darkest corner of Hell. His shard, the bit of his soul that knew when his fated mate was near.

One more second and he was either dead or...nope, probably just dead. How could fate do this to him now?

Fuck fate. He believed in the power of hope. He and his brethren never would have survived Hell without having hope that they would someday be saved. He had to hold onto that now. His life unshackled from the darkness was only just beginning, and this was not how it would end.

His wing caught on a tree that was too big to snap and he crashed face first into the ground. He rolled head over ass, skidding to a stop embedded deep into the ground and trees. His mind and vision went foggy and he pulled on that power of hope that he would wake up.

The last thing he heard before he closed his eyes and faded into an unconscious limbo was a soft, lyrical voice. *That's right, Neo. Keep that hope alive. Your mate could use a dose of hope too.*

He sunk into the dark oblivion of pain. But there in the darkness was one more voice, this one laughing...at him. *Why are all my sons such douchecanoes? I guess crashing into the side of a mountain is one way to get your mate's attention. Oh goodie, look, light of my heart. here she comes. You've chosen well for him.*

The lyrical voice laughed. *Of course I have. They're perfect for each other.*

Remember son, lots and lots of orgasms is the best way to please your mate.

Get Tamed now to keep reading in Kindle Unlimited, ebook, paperback, and audiobook.

ACKNOWLEDGMENTS

I'm so grateful for my Mushrooms, Jenny Madore, Bri Blackwood, Claudia Burgoa, M. Guida, and Dylann Crush, and my Amazeballs Writers - Danielle Hart, Stephanie Harrell, Davina Storm, and Cara Bryant who are always willing to get on and do writing sprints with me. I appreciate it more than you could know, and am infinitely proud of your successes in publishing.

My Amazeballs Facebook group is so much of the reason I keep writing and I look forward to logging onto the FaceSpace every day and seeing what kind of fun and games we've got going on!

Big thanks to my proofreader, Chrisandra. She probably hates commas as much as I do now. All the remaining errors are all my fault. I'm sure I screwed it up somewhere.

I'm ever grateful to Elli Zafiris and Becca Syme for telling me I'm worth fighting for when I'm sure I've effed up my book and my career. You two are my energy pennies.

I am so very grateful to have readers who will join my on my crazy book adventures where there will ALWAYS be curvy girls getting happy ever afters!

Without all of you, I wouldn't be able to feed my cats (or live the dream of a creative life!)

Special thanks to everyone who went through the weird cover fiasco with me and supported my use of a real, plus-size, ba-donka donka curvy girl on the individual book covers of the Fate of the Wolf Guard series.

It was a risk to put a woman on the cover who wasn't a drawing, and wasn't what society thinks of as the ideal body. It's a risk I was willing to take for all the curvy girls out there who've been told or thought they weren't deserving of love because of your size, shape, or what the scale says.

Yes. You. Are.

Thank you so much to all my Patreon Book Dragons!

An enormous thanks to my Official Biggest Fans Ever. You're the best book dragons a curvy girl author could ask for~

Thank you so much for all your undying devotion for me and the characters I write. You keep me writing (almost) every day.

Hugs and Kisses and Signed Books and Swag for you from me! I am so incredibly grateful for each of you and am awed by your support.

- Helena E.
- Alida H.
- Daphine G.
- Bridget M.
- Stephanie F.
- Danielle T.
- Marea H.
- Marilyn C.
- Mari G.
- Cherie S.
- Jessica W.
- Katherine M.
- Kelli W.
- Stephanie H.

Shout out to my Official VIP Fans!
Extra Hugs and to you ~

- Jeanette M.

- Kerrie M.
- Michele C.
- Corinne A.
- Deborah S.
- Frania G.
- Jennifer B.
- Hannah P.
- Janice M.
- Nicole W.
- Sandra B.
- Sherrie W.
- DebbieJoy G.
- Heather R.
- Janice W.
- Robin O.

Dragons Love Curves

Chase Me

Tease Me

Unmask Me

Bite Me

Cage Me

Baby Me

Defy Me

Surprise Me

Dirty Dragon

Crave Me

Dragon Love Letters - Curvy Connection Exclusive

Slay Me

Play Me

Merry Me

The Black Dragon Brotherhood

Tamed

Tangled

Twisted

Fated For Curves

A Touch of Fate

A Tangled Fate

A Twist of Fate

Alpha Wolves Want Curves

Dirty Wolf

Naughty Wolf

Kinky Wolf

Hungry Wolf

Flirty Wolf - Curvy Connection Exclusive

Grumpy Wolves

Filthy Wolf

The Fate of the Wolf Guard

Unclaimed

Untamed

Undone

Undefeated

Claimed by the Seven Realms

Protected

Stolen

Crowned

By Aidy Award and Piper Fox

Big Wolf on Campus

Cocky Jock Wolf

Bad Boy Wolf

Heart Throb Wolf

Hot Shot Wolf

———————————

Contemporary Romance by Aidy Award

The Curvy Love Series

Curvy Diversion

Curvy Temptation

Curvy Persuasion

The Curvy Seduction Saga

Rebound

Rebellion

Reignite

Rejoice

Revel

ABOUT THE AUTHOR

Aidy Award is a curvy girl who kind of has a thing for stormtroopers. She's also the author of the popular Curvy Love series and the hot new Dragons Love Curves series.

She writes curvy girl erotic romance, about real love, and dirty fun, with happy ever afters because every woman deserves great sex and even better romance, no matter her size, shape, or what the scale says.

Read the delicious tales of hot heroes and curvy heroines come to life under the covers and between the pages of Aidy's books. Then let her know because she really does want to hear from her readers.

Connect with Aidy on her website.

www.AidyAward.com get her Curvy Connection, and join her Facebook Group - Aidy's Amazeballs.

Printed in Great Britain
by Amazon